ZOEY'S MEMORY

By Sara Kate

COPYRIGHT

TABLE OF CONTENTS

CHAPTER 1

DEC 11th

5:00 A.M.

Why is my head hurting? Whose bed is this? Where am I?

Zoey struggled to sit up in the twin-sized bed she woke up in. Her body ached, her head pounded, and her hair was slightly damp. The room was almost completely dark except for a dull light that shone through a small window in front of her. She could hear the pouring rain outside, but she could not see it through the window. A thin gown covered her body, one that she was not familiar with.

Why am I wearing this?

She swung her feet off the edge of the bed, and as they dropped to the carpeted floor, it felt like two bricks were attached to them. She stood up, feeling lightheaded, and stumbled over to the light, her feet hurting with every step.

As Zoey got closer to the window, she realized it was on a door. Stepping on to her tiptoes, she peered out. A long hallway stretched both to the left and right side of the door, colored by light blue walls. A row of black doors with more windows were spread throughout, almost resembling an indoor apartment building. She cautiously turned the doorknob and poked her head through the doorway before stepping out.

"He-- Hello?" she asked to no one in particular.

Where the hell am I?

Zoey took a step into the hallway. The light was causing her headache to become so severe; she could barely keep her eyes open. So, she had to use her hands to maneuver against the walls.

Why do I have such a terrible headache?

Just as she was about to reach the next door, the hall began to spin so she stopped to close her eyes.

Why do I feel like this?

Suddenly, Zoey felt a strong hand grab her left shoulder. "HEY! WHAT THE HELL!" she cried out as she turned around. "I found her. Yeah, I'm taking her back now," a tall man with a bodybuilder figure said into a radio.

A woman's voice on the other side of it came back a second later. "Copy that, Tee. Thank you."

Zoey went to pull away but just as she did, a sharp pain rushed through her body and the hallway started to become blurry. She looked down towards the pain, just in time to see Tee pulling a large needle out of her right arm.

"What the-" Zoey couldn't even finish her sentence before passing right out.

11:00 A.M.

"Wake up," Tee said, as he threw a plastic bag on Zoey's bed. She pulled the covers off her head, feeling groggy. "What's going on?" she asked as she sat up slowly.

"Shower's in the corner. Toothbrush and paste are on the sink." His voice was deep and monotone as he pointed in the direction of the tiny bathroom in the corner of the room. "Get dressed. Dr. Hall's waiting for you."

"Who?" Zoey asked, confused. She surveyed the room with her eyes. Besides the bathroom, the only thing in it, other than the bed she woke up in was a nightstand with a lamp on top of it. There were no windows besides the small one on the door.

"Get dressed," Tee repeated, then walked into the hallway and stood in front of her door, leaving it open.

What is going on?

Zoey opened the bag and pulled out a pair of sweatpants and a large black T-shirt, which was greatly oversized for her five-foot-four body. She went to the bathroom to change. It was a small bathroom, with just a sink, mirror, toilet and shower without a tub. She closed the door behind her and went to lock it but there wasn't one.

Where am I?

When she put the clothes on, the shirt reached to her knees and the sweatpants were baggy but fit just enough to not fall down her waist. She looked at herself in the mirror and saw that her normally thin shoulder-length black hair was tangled all over.

"What happened to me?" she asked herself out loud as she ran her fingers through her hair to try to separate the knots.

"Let's go," Tee called.

Zoey stopped messing with her hair and walked out of the bathroom to find Tee still standing at the doorway of her room. When he saw her, he immediately grabbed her by the arm.

"You don't have to hold my hand," she snapped, trying to pull away.

"Good to know," he muttered as he slightly eased his grip.

She followed him down the left of the hallway. They passed eight other rooms with the same black doors and small windows like the one that Zoey woke up in. Most of the doors were open and she could see people in the rooms wearing hospital gowns and pajamas, either sleeping or lingering by the doorways.

"WHERE AM I?" Zoey demanded.

Instead of answering, Tee continued to lead her down the hall.

Just as they were about to make a right turn, the very last door flung open. A tall young man with dark brown straight shoulder length hair poked his head out of the doorway, then took one large step out in front of Zoey. She jumped back, startled, which made him laugh hysterically.

"Welcome to the club! The demons are coming... they're coming!" he laughed as he threw his head back and forth.

"Back in your room!" Tee said, sternly.

The boy yelled loudly, as if Tee just attacked him, then hunched down to the ground.

Wherever I am… I don't belong here…

Tee tugged Zoey's arm and she continued to follow him around the corner, keeping her eyes on the crouched boy now sitting on the floor.

Distracted by him, she bumped right into a very thin girl who was just a bit taller than her.

The girl's thick black curls bounced against her shoulders as she skipped backward toward Zoey. "Excuse you, newbie!" she said, smiling in a way that Zoey could not tell if it was fake or not.

"Uh, hi?" Zoey said as more of a question than a greeting.

"Ignore everyone. Let's go. Dr. Hall's on a schedule," Tee interrupted.

"Who the hell is Dr. Hall?" Zoey asked but again, he ignored her and pulled her away.

"See you soon," the girl smirked, then skipped back down the hall.

"WHERE AM I?!" Zoey demanded again, now growing more aggravated. She tried to let loose of Tee's grip, but he tightened it and continued to nearly drag her down the hall.

They passed another hallway, which looked like it connected back to Zoey's room, so she decided to run down it but had no luck as Tee quickly picked her up and threw her over his shoulder.

"PUT ME DOWN! WHAT IS GOING ON? WHY WON'T YOU ANSWER ME!?" she yelled as she fought in his arms.

He continued to carry her until he reached the end of the hall and stopped in front of a door that sat across from a big desk. The desk was protected by glass and three nurses were sitting behind it. Tee put her down and held her by one arm while he knocked on the door. Zoey stopped struggling as she was now too fixated on the prison-like desk behind her.

"Come in!" a woman called out a moment later from behind the door.

Tee held the door open for Zoey, allowing her to walk in first.

She stepped into a small office where two tall bookshelves stacked with psychology and mental health books decorated the walls. A big window was placed behind a woman, who was holding a phone to her ear. She said goodbye to whoever was on the other line and stood up from her chair. As she did, Zoey immediately noticed her bright red lips. They matched perfectly with her cherry-red pixie cut and dark red blush.

"Hi Zoey, my name is Dr. Hall. Do you remember arriving here?" she asked in a friendly tone.

Zoey shook her head while inspecting the room with her eyes. "No… Where am I?"

"Why don't you sit down?" Dr. Hall gestured towards the wood chair in front of her desk.

"No. Tell me what's going on first!" Zoey resisted.

Dr. Hall sat back down and gave Zoey a very sincere look.

"Okay, Zoey. You were brought here by the police at 3:00 a.m. this morning shortly after you ran into the police station. You were yelling and acting violently towards the officers. You were very distraught," Dr. Hall paused, "Zoey, please take a seat."

"Uh- uh... wh--what are you talking about?" Zoey stuttered as she gripped tightly on to the back of the chair, still standing. She cautiously looked around the room, feeling more confused than she ever thought to imagine.

WHAT DID SHE JUST SAY? IS THIS A JOKE?!

"Zoey, please take a seat," Dr. Hall said again, calmly.

"And what exactly was I yelling?" Zoey asked in disbelief.

Dr. Hall gave her a hard stare before answering.

"It sounded like you were very concerned about your mother being alive."

Yeah, this must be a joke... and it's not funny.

"Okay... you've got the wrong person. I definitely didn't do that," Zoey said. She turned to walk out of the door. "I'm just going to go-"

"Zoey," Dr. Hall interrupted, "it's important that you sit and listen to what you did. Do you remember anything at all? What about this morning? Do you remember waking up a few hours after you arrived here?"

"You mean before your guard dog sedated me and locked me up? Then yes. Yes, I do remember that." Zoey sat down in anger.

"What is this place? Why did I have to come here?"

Dr. Hall opened the laptop on her desk while Zoey sat impatiently, legs shaking in her seat. She typed for a moment, then turned the laptop to the side so both her and Zoey could see the screen. She clicked on a video that was posted on a social media site, then set it to full screen.

What in the world?

Zoey's heart began pounding so fast, that it felt like the sound of it was audible to the room. She leaned in closer and squinted her eyes to see the screen better.

That can't be me...

The status below the video on the screen read: **FLORIDA WOMAN RAN INTO THE POLICE STATION CLAIMING MOTHER IS STILL ALIVE**.

Dr. Hall played the video, which revealed Zoey looking extremely distraught, screaming the words *my mom's alive* repeatedly in front of the police station.

OH MY GOD... HOW THE HELL IS THAT ME?

Dr. Hall closed the laptop. "You are in the Behavioral section of Regional Hospital. Now, do you believe me?"

Zoey's eyes and mouth were wide open, in shock. She was nearly speechless.

I don't remember doing that at all...

Dr. Hall handed her a pocket-sized notebook. "Here is your daily schedule."

"Wait... you-- you still didn't tell me what happened!" Zoey shook her head, confused.

"You just saw it, Zoey," Dr. Hall said, nodding towards the laptop.

"No- no... but... but why did I do that?"

"I don't know Zoey, but I'm sure we'll figure it out together," Dr. Hall smiled.

"Is this a joke?" Zoey asked in disbelief. Her mind was racing.

Dr. Hall shook her head, still holding an annoyingly positive smile. "I'm sorry, Zoey. It is not a joke."

"I don't even remember doing that... I don't remember anything..." Zoey mumbled.

Dr. Hall stood up and walked around the desk, towards her. "It's okay. That is what these daily sessions are for," she said as she pointed to the notebook. "They are going to help discuss what's going on with you and how you're feeling."

"How I'm feeling?" Zoey asked skeptically. "I want to know why I did that! I must have been drugged or something... this doesn't make sense..."

"Well, we did take your blood when you came in and no drugs were found in your system. There was only a small trace of alcohol," Dr. Hall said, "but I don't think alcohol was the reason for your actions. There wasn't enough of it in your system to cause you to lose functionality."

Loose functionality?

Zoey tried to speak but all she could do was stutter. "I-I- no, this can't... this can't be right..."

"We're going to figure this out. That is why the police brought you to us," Dr. Hall said.

"Bu-- but why would they bring me here? I am not insane... I know who I am...I..." Zoey stammered.

"You kept insisting that your mother was alive, Zoey. The police asked you to call someone that could pick you up, but you would not give them anyone's number. They felt you might have been more of a danger to yourself if they sent you home alone... so that's why you're here," Dr. Hall said as she walked over to the door. "I'm here to help you, Zoey. Now, why don't you go get acquainted with your surroundings? The cafeteria's just down the hall to the left," she said as she held open her office door.

Zoey slowly stood up, still in shock.

"You'll be okay. I promise," Dr. Hall said in a reassuring tone.

"So... so when can I go home?" Zoey asked as she started to walk towards the door.

"Not until you're ready. I need to make sure that you are not a danger to yourself or anyone else anymore," Dr. Hall said.

They really think I'm dangerous...

"Uh, are you serious? You're honestly telling me that I can't leave on my own?" Zoey asked, stunned.

Dr. Hall raised both eyebrows.

"And you're telling me that I should let you go home after seeing yourself in that video?"

I don't know what I just saw of myself...

"I- uh, okay, whatever..." Zoey mumbled and walked out of the office.

I woke up in a psych ward… I don't remember anything I did yesterday… how the hell did I do this to myself?

She looked down at her daily schedule. It read:

DAILY SCHEDULE:
7:00 a.m. - 9:00 a.m. Breakfast
12:00 p.m. - 1:30 p.m. Lunch
2:00 p.m. Activity Time
5:00 p.m. Daily Session
6:00 p.m. - 8:00 p.m. Dinner
9:00 p.m. Bedtime

You've got to be kidding me…

"Hi!" The girl who bumped into Zoey earlier was suddenly standing behind her. She looked Zoey up and down as she held both hands on her hips.

"I'm Destiny. You're the new girl Zoey, right?!" she asked with a smile so wide it looked like it hurt.

"Yeah… how do you know my name?" Zoey asked, cautiously.

"Nothing gets past me here! I know everything! Come on, I'll show you where lunch is!" Destiny started to skip away, pulling Zoey by the hand along with her.

They took a left down the first hallway where Zoey initially tried to escape from Tee and stopped in front of the first door on the right. Destiny stood with her arms spread open like she was Vanna White. "So, this is the activity room!" she cheered.

Zoey poked her head through the doorway. There was an old couch that looked like it could fit about three or four people directly in the middle of the room. It faced a medium-sized flat screen television with a stack of DVDs in the drawers of the TV stand under it. The sun shined through a window with bars across it, in the far-left corner of the room. A telephone hung on the wall a few feet next to it and two long tables, with foldable chairs were placed nearby. There were two desks next to each other in the right corner of the room. One had a board game on top of it and the other had crayons and paper. Some yoga mats were scattered on the floor.

Zoey went to walk in, but Destiny stretched her arm across the doorway.

"Let's not go in until activity time. It's about to be lunch anyways," she said.

"And what do we do during activity time?" Zoey groaned.

"It's when we do activities, duh! You know... games, TV, drawing, yoga. Time where we're supposed to have fun and be kind to one another." Destiny rolled her eyes.

"We do group circles sometimes too. It's more like group therapy... without calling it group therapy. It's on your schedule, ya know." She gave Zoey a curious look.

"So, what if we don't want to do activity time?" Zoey sighed.

"You have to do activity time! If you don't how up, Dr. Hall's going to say that you're not making progress and mark it down in your chart. Then she'll give you the speech," Destiny said as she rolled her eyes and air quoted, "you have to socialize and talk about your feelings with others to get past your problems and blah blah blah… anywho, let's keep going."

"And how long have you been here, Destiny?" Zoey asked as she started to follow her.

Destiny stopped skipping and turned towards Zoey. Her body became stiff and her smile dropped.

"I first got here not long after grandma died," she said in a low tone.

"Oh. I'm sorry to hear-"

"Anywho!" Destiny's voice perked up as she flipped her hair and took a deep breath, "let's go eat!"

I wonder if she killed grandma...

They walked into the next room which was just a bit bigger than the activity room.

"This is the cafeteria," Destiny said as they stepped in.

The room had six circular tables and a buffet line in the back, reminding Zoey of a high school cafeteria.

"AH! NOOOOO!!! THEY'RE COMING TO GET ALL OF US! ALL OF US!" the patient who jumped in front of Zoey earlier, yelled out from one of the tables.

Tee and another big bulky guy in uniform came running past the girls towards him, causing Zoey to jump.

"That's just Derek, he does that sometimes," Destiny said, nonchalantly.

Okay... I need to get myself out of here now...

Zoey watched the guards grab Derek's arms and stabilize him at the table. His screams suddenly started to fall quiet.

"COME ON GIRL!" Destiny whined, pulling Zoey to the lunch line.

I need to get away from this girl...

They got in line and the lady behind the food line slapped a burger with a slice of cold American cheese and fries on their plates.

Zoey followed Destiny over to a table where two pale skinned girls with blue eyes were playing with a deck of cards. They looked very much alike, almost like twins, but one looked to be just a few years older than the other. They both had bleach blonde wavy hair and clearly hadn't brushed it in days. The younger girl wore her hair in a high ponytail and the other girl wore it loose, which reached to the middle of her back.

"It's my turn! Not yours!" the younger girl yelled.

"No, it was my turn!" the older girl yelled back as she chucked the deck of cards across the table and then ran out of the cafeteria. The other girl ran right after her.

"That was Lisa and Tina. They're sisters," Destiny said with a mouthful of her burger.

"Tina's 25. Lisa's 21."

"Lisa looks like she's still 18," Zoey remarked.

"Yeah, she has that baby face that every woman wishes she has. Their parents were drug addicts and then they got put into the system when Tina was 17. Oh man, that made Tina so mad!" Destiny lowered her head and whispered, "they started a fire at one of their foster homes. That's when they got sent away to a hospital like this somewhere in Miami. They got transferred to this one only a couple months ago."

So, they're arsonists… I'm in a hospital with adult children and arsonists.

"Why did they get transferred here?" Zoey asked, poking at the cold burger bun on her plate.

"Lisa told me that Tina tried to stab another patient and then Lisa tried to stop them from fighting and then bam!" Destiny flicked her hands in the air. "They got transferred."

"Did anyone get hurt in that fire?" Zoey questioned.

"That's a good question," Destiny shrugged.

This can't be real life…

"Nothing is making any sense right now… I shouldn't be in here," Zoey mumbled to herself out loud.

"Nothing ever makes any sense, Zo Zo," Destiny said as she finished off the last of her fries.

For a skinny girl, she sure ate a lot and quickly too.

"Uh," Zoey paused, "call me Zoey."

After pondering for a moment, Destiny shook her head. "Nah, I like Zo Zo."

Choosing to ignore it, Zoey tried to eat but couldn't stomach the taste.

"I can't eat any more of this. I'm getting nauseous," she said.

"It's probably because of the meds they gave you last night. They give it to everybody, no matter who you are or what your problem is," Destiny sighed. She took the last few bites of her burger, clearing the plate, then got up with her tray. "Well let's go introduce you to the others."

I don't want to see the others... I want to get the hell out of here.

Zoey got up and followed Destiny, not sure why she was doing so.

They went down the hallway, passing patients who were either talking, laughing, or crying to themselves. Lisa and Tina were sitting cross-legged on the floor, playing cards outside of what Zoey expected was their room. This time neither were yelling at each other. They were so focused on their game, that they ignored Destiny when she said hello to them.

"I'll introduce you later. They take their games VERY SERIOUSLY," Destiny whispered as they walked by.

"So, if we keep going down this hall, it will wrap around back to where your room is," she said, turning around to go back the way they came from. "Now, let me show you where my room is."

I need to escape this girl...

She led Zoey back down the hallway and walked into a room just a few doors before Dr. Hall's office.

"Oh, let me show you my art! I'm an artist, did you know!?" Destiny exclaimed.

Zoey stood at the doorway, hesitant to walk in.

"Come in silly," Destiny persisted.

Zoey slowly walked in. Destiny's room looked just like hers but instead was decorated with paper drawings and paintings on the walls. There was a large pile of clothes on the floor. The bed was the same size as Zoey's and a bathroom was placed in the corner of the room, as well.

Destiny held up a piece of paper with five large red stars painted on it. "Do you like it?" she asked eagerly.

"Uh, yeah... it looks nice," Zoey said uncomfortably. "Um, it's nice of you to show me around but I think I'm going to go back to my room... I need to uh, settle in."

Destiny looked at her with sad eyes and sighed, "okay, Zo Zo. I understand. I'll give you some space! See you later!"

Zoey awkwardly smiled and hurried out of Destiny's room.

Okay, I need to figure out how to get out of this place...

She headed down the first hallway, where Lisa and Tina were sitting and took the turn to get back to her room.

When she got there, Zoey closed the door behind her and let out a deep sigh. *Okay... okay, stay calm. I need to figure this out. There has got to be a misunderstanding or something...*

She started pacing in her room. Her heart was beating rapidly, and her mind raced as she couldn't recall anything that Dr. Hall showed her on video.

I need to call Alex... can I even call someone? Am I allowed? Why didn't I ask? Why didn't I tell the police to call Alex?

Zoey pulled her little notebook out of the pocket of her sweatpants and looked at the daily schedule on the first page.

"2:00 p.m. Activity time. Session 5:00 p.m. What is this crap?" She tossed the notebook across the room in anger.

Now, she was beginning to hyperventilate, and the room was beginning to feel like it was caving in on her. For the first time in a good year, Zoey could feel a panic attack coming on. "I can't stay in this room," she gasped.

The clock on the wall showed ten minutes until two in the afternoon. So, she rushed out of her room and towards the activity room.

When she got there, Destiny immediately walked up behind her, startling Zoey once again. "You get scared a lot," she laughed.

That's because you creep up on people like a serial killer.

"Are we allowed to use the phone?" Zoey asked, ignoring her comment.

"Oh yeah, of course. You can use it anytime," Destiny happily answered.

"Thanks," Zoey muttered and went over to the phone.

After a few rings, Alex didn't answer so she left a voicemail. "Hey sis, it's me. So, uh, I'm in a psych ward, well it's the behavioral section of the hospital... um, anyway, I need you to get me out... I don't really understand or remember getting here... but they won't let me leave... I'm okay though. Uh, anyways call me back on this number when you get this message... love you."

I hope she checks her voicemails... I wonder if she already knows what happened...

Zoey hung up the phone and went over to go look out of the window.

She looked down at a courtyard which only had a small garden and a bench nearby and a fence with barbed wire ran around the perimeter of the yard. Zoey figured she was on the second floor as the ground didn't seem too far from her view. She looked at the gloomy sky, then exchanged her gaze back to the activity room.

Lisa and Tina sat across from each other at the table, playing cards. Derek was lying on the ground, flat on his stomach, coloring like a child although he looked to be at least in his mid-twenties. Two other male patients were attempting yoga on the mats, while a girl with long greasy brunette hair sang the song *let it go*, and a sinister-looking male sat quietly on the couch, staring at the TV.

What am I doing here with these people?

Suddenly, it started becoming difficult for Zoey to catch her breath and she began feeling overwhelmed. She could feel a panic attack coming on again, so she knelt on her knees and dropped her head in her hands.

Now's not the time for this... I must be strong... this hasn't happened in so long... it can't start happening now!

Zoey started getting panic attacks three years after her mother died. It was like hell had fallen on her every time one came on and she was glad that she hadn't encountered one in a whole year. The fact that she could feel them coming back now was beginning to anger her.

"Are you okay, Zo Zo?" Destiny's perky voice took Zoey out of her thoughts.

"Uh, yeah, yeah, I'm fine," Zoey said. She quickly stood up and wiped her eyes.

I can't be weak here.

"How long is activity time?" she asked.

"For an hour or two. It just depends on how long you want to stay... but remember, they're watching." Destiny nudged her head towards a friendly looking nurse, who was now walking their way.

"Hi, Zoey. My name is Debra. I'm the activity room nurse," she said. "We have some board games and some coloring books over on the table. I'm here if you need anything."

What I need is to get out of here!

"Thanks," Zoey muttered.

Debra nodded happily, then walked over to another patient.

Zoey went to sit on the couch next to the guy who looked hypnotized by the TV screen, along with Destiny who dropped herself right in between them. She scooted herself as close as she could to the young man and batted her eyes.

"Hi, Will. You like the movie so far?" she giggled.

Someone has a crush.

He ignored her, so she repeated her question.

"Yes. Destiny," he replied, clearly annoyed as he continued to stare straight.

"Cool!" her voice squeaked. "Oh! I didn't introduce you two yet! This is Zo Zo."

Zoey rolled her eyes. "It's Zoey, not Zo Zo."

"Cool," he muttered.

For the next hour of the movie, Destiny did not talk at all, which Zoey was grateful for. She needed the quiet as her mind wandered. She was beginning to feel like she couldn't think straight anymore. All her thoughts overlapped, and it was hard to just focus on one thing.

Why did I run to the cops? My mom is dead. None of this is making sense...

Lost in her thoughts, Zoey didn't even realize the movie ended until Destiny stood up from the couch.

"What a funny movie! Ah, I'm going to go take a nap. I'm sleepy now," she yawned. "I'll see you at Dinner, Zo Zo!"

Destiny left the room, leaving Zoey alone on the couch with Will, who was still staring at the now blank television screen.

"The movie's over..." she said.

Instead of answering her, he huffed, then got up from the couch.

"Alright, then..." Zoey muttered.

She pulled out her notebook and looked at the wall clock which only read a quarter past three.

5:00 p.m. *Daily Session next... lovely.*

5:00 P.M.

"What is the last thing you remember before waking up here?" Dr. Hall asked Zoey, who was fidgeting in her seat.

"I don't know, you tell me. You seem to have all the answers," Zoey snapped.

"I'm not here for your attitude. I'm here to help you," Dr. Hall said, still smiling. "What do you do for a living, Zoey?"

"I'm a photographer."

"Oh, what do you photograph?"

"Weddings and family portraits," Zoey sighed.

Dr. Hall typed on her laptop for a moment then asked, "any brothers or sisters?"

Zoey shook her head.

"Have you had a chance to call anyone yet? You're free to dial out at any time and have people call you as well."

"Yeah, thanks for telling me that before..."

"You didn't allow me to really tell you much of anything, Zoey," Dr. Hall responded.

Zoey rolled her eyes. "I called my sister... Alex, but she didn't answer."

"I thought you just said no to when I asked you about having siblings?" Dr. Hall questioned.

"Alex is my best friend. I call her my sister because we've been friends for like 12 years. We're basically siblings at this point," Zoey shrugged.

"Oh okay, I understand," Dr. Hall nodded, "I have a best friend that's like my sister too. We've been friends for almost as long as you and Alex have... oh, I believe it's been about ten years for us now."

Cut the small talk and send me home.

"So, is Alex the only person close to you?" Dr. Hall continued.

"Uh-huh," Zoey mumbled as she grew impatient.

"When you arrived at the station you seemed concerned about your mother being alive, but you wouldn't cooperate with the police," Dr. Hall said, changing the subject quickly.

"That's because my mom is dead," Zoey said dryly.

"I understand and I'm deeply sorry to hear that. Do you mind if I ask what she died from?"

Here we go, with the dead parent story.

Zoey looked down towards her feet and sighed, "cancer. She died ten years ago."

"That must have been awfully hard on you. Especially at the age of 15," Dr. Hall said.

Zoey looked up from her lap. "What, how do you know that?"

"Well, you're 25 now, so by the math…"

"How do you know my age? I never told you that," Zoey asked.

"I saw your birthdate on your license, Zoey. It was in your purse. I promise I'm just here to help you," Dr. Hall said kindly. "I have no false intentions here."

She put her hands in the air as if she were under arrest.

"Then why didn't you tell me that you had my license this whole time? Where is my purse then? Do you have it?" Zoey crossed her arms.

"I didn't think it was that important and yes, I do have your purse. You had it on you

30

when you went into the station... Didn't you see it in the video?"

"I'm not sure what I saw," Zoey murmured.

"What was her name?" Dr. Hall asked.

"Who?" Zoey shook her head, confused.

"Your mother," Dr. Hall said.

"Her name was Leanne," Zoey said softly.

Dr. Hall typed again before speaking.

"Are you currently going through any type of support or therapy for her death?"

Zoey gave her an odd look. "It was ten years ago. I don't need support now..."

Dr. Hall continued, "have you ever gone through any type of therapy for her death?"

"Nope. Never needed it," Zoey answered hastily. She looked around at all the different mental health books and started feeling more aggravated.

"Did you have a good relationship with her?" Dr. Hall continued as she typed.

"Yup," Zoey shifted in her seat. "So how are these questions going to help me figure out what happened?"

"Well, I don't know anything about you so usually, I like to start with getting to know you by hearing about your background... and well, you were very concerned about your mother being alive which is why you're sitting here right now. So, I'd like to hear and understand a bit more about your childhood to help you figure out what's going on with your mental."

My mental?

"No, no, no. That's okay," Zoey said. She stood up and waved her hand. "I have never needed therapy and I don't need it now. Sorry, but I don't like talking to strangers about my life." She pushed the chair in and turned to walk out of the door. "I don't even know why I'm talking to you, so good-"

"Zoey," Dr. Hall interrupted.

"Oh my god! What?!" Zoey nearly shouted out of anger.

Dr. Hall stood up from her desk. "Our session today can be over, but we will have to talk about this again."

"When can I leave here?" Zoey groaned.

"When I feel that you aren't a danger to yourself or anyone else," Dr. Hall said.

This can't really be happening to me...

"So, I can't check myself out of here at all... at any time, whatsoever?"

"No, I'm sorry but it's for your best interest," Dr. Hall said.

"There's got to be a misunderstanding... this is ridiculous..." Zoey muttered as she flung the door open and stormed out of the office.

Just as she was on her way back to her room, Destiny popped out of her room.

Why is this girl everywhere?

"My girl, Zo Zo! Where ya going?!" she asked, full of cheer.

"Just heading back to my room so I can sit in some peace before dinner," Zoey said through gritted teeth.

I just want to be left alone...

"Dinner's in like 30 minutes, silly. You're gonna do nothing in 30 minutes, come with me!"

"That's the point," Zoey sighed.

Destiny skipped towards the cafeteria, pulling Zoey along with her. "Oh, let's finish our tour! So, you saw Dr. Hall's office already and the nurses' station and the entrance obviously, so let's go-"

"Entrance? Where? I didn't see an entrance."

Zoey looked back down the hallway towards Dr. Hall's office.

"Yeah, it's right behind the nurse's station on the other side, through the double doors... I've never seen that side," Destiny said sadly.

And you probably never will...

As Zoey followed behind Destiny, she spotted the girl with the long scraggly hair who was singing earlier. She was now jumping up and down in the hall, resembling a crackhead that desperately needed her fix.

"That's Kelsey. Be careful around her. She's crazier than Hannibal on bath salts," Destiny gripped on to Zoey's wrist as they got closer and whispered, "don't make eye contact."

Zoey used her peripherals as they quickly walked by Kelsey.

"So, what's her story?"

"Kelsey's brother committed her here almost a year ago, I think. She had a drug problem in her twenties, she's in her thirties now... such an old woman," Destiny shook her head, "such a shame... I am never going to look that way when I get that age. I'm 19 now, FYI! Anywho, Kelsey was into a bunch of drugs then she got sober for a year... did drugs again and then started telling people that she was seeing ghosts which freaked her brother out. So, he dumped Kelsey here. I mean, I believe in my grandma being a spirit ghost but not a bad one... I see my grandma sometimes at night before I fall asleep, and it makes me happy. I think Kelsey sees bad ghosts."

She stopped in front of a locked door with no window in the middle of the hallway that circled back to Zoey's room.

"Uh, what are we doing?" Zoey asked skeptically.

"This is the basement. No one's allowed to go down here because it's locked," Destiny whispered.

"There's no basement in Florida," Zoey shook her head.

You are with crazy people... don't forget.

"There is in this building," Destiny persisted.

"Okay... uh, and what happens in the basement?" Zoey questioned.

"We don't know," Destiny said dramatically, "as long as I've been here, I can't tell you anyway."

Just as Zoey was trying to rationalize what Destiny said, Tee's voice made her jump.

"Dinner time, ladies," he said while standing with his arms crossed behind them.

For god's sake, if it's not Destiny, it's Tee.

"You heard the sexy man," Destiny giggled.

She twirled her curly hair and batted her eyes.

Tee raised one eyebrow, unamused.

I need to get myself out of here tonight...

6:00 P.M.

After the cafeteria lady dumped a plate full of mashed potatoes and chicken on Destiny and Zoey's plates, they went to sit with Lisa and Tina.

"Hey ladies!" Destiny said cheerfully as she sat down in front of the sisters.

"Hi," they both replied in unison.

"I didn't get to introduce you to my new friend, here. Her name is Zo Zo. She came in last night."

"Hi, Zo Zo," Lisa pointed to her sister, "this is Tina! I'm Lisa!"

"Actually, it's Zoey, not Zo Zo," Zoey said, correcting her.

"So why are you here?" Tina asked.

Common question.

"Well, I don't know... Hopefully, I'll find out soon..."

"We can help you!" Lisa volunteered, eagerly.

"NO!" Tina said sternly, "we cannot."

Zoey shook her head. "No, that's fine. I don't need anyone's help. I'm sure I'll figure it out."

She picked with her fork at the lumpy potatoes topped with sour cream and butter on her plate and then took a bite of the chicken which tasted bland with absolutely no flavoring.

As she played with her food, Zoey noticed Tina who was stabbing the chicken forcefully with her fork.

"What did that chicken do to you?" Zoey sarcastically asked.

35

Tina dropped her fork and glared at Zoey.

I probably shouldn't joke around here.

"It's what these people do!" Tina snarked. "They're never going to let us free. They don't think we're old enough to take care of ourselves! It's stupid!"

"I see... uh, I," Zoey stuttered, not sure how to respond.

"Tina's mad because they won't let her have guardianship of me," Lisa added, "ever since that stupid fire..."

"SH!" Tina hissed.

"Anywho," Destiny said, changing the subject. "Have any of you seen Will?"

She looked around the cafeteria intently. "I want to have a little chat with him!"

I don't think Will feels the same way... I need to get away from these girls...

Zoey took a few more bites of her food then told the girls that she was going to lay down in her room.

She left the cafeteria, feeling lost, scared, confused, and all in between as she just couldn't shake the image of herself on video and the scary feeling of not remembering why.

I just need to remember why I did that and prove to Dr. Hall that I'm not dangerous... Then I can go home... this will be over soon.

CHAPTER 2

DEC 12th

7:00 A.M.

Between the noises from the other patients and nurses, along with the thunder and rain outside the hospital, Zoey tossed and turned all night. In total, she had only received an hour and a half of sleep. Her eyes had wandered over to the bathroom shower every now and then, yearning to step in but she fought the temptation as she feared someone would come into her room. Since there was no lock on the door, she didn't want to chance it.

Although, Zoey saw herself on video, she was not sure why she was in the hospital, especially the psych ward. After meeting the other patients yesterday, it was clear that she did not belong. She didn't know why the doctor couldn't see that, and she was even more confused about how to make her. After a few hours of brainstorming, the only thing Zoey could recall before first waking up in the hospital was waking up at home.

There's got to be something wrong with me… why the hell would I only forget one day?

Fearing that something could seriously be wrong with her brain, Zoey started to make a list of what she did know, hoping it would control her mind.

-I am a photographer.

-I have a sister named Alex.

-My mom has been dead for ten years. My dad is still alive.

-I woke up in a psych ward of a hospital yesterday morning.

-I don't know what happened the day before beside waking up, drinking coffee, and reading for a little while.

-Today's date is December-

"Wait, what is today's date?" Zoey asked herself as she looked at the clock in her room.

It showed just a few minutes past seven in the morning, which according to her schedule, breakfast was starting to be served. However, instead of going to eat Zoey decided to go straight to Dr. Hall's office.

She hurried down the hallway and knocked repeatedly until Dr. Hall opened the door.

"Good morning, Zoey. How are you doing?" Dr. Hall asked as she gestured for Zoey to come in.

"I'd be a lot better if I knew why I was here. I have a few questions for you," Zoey said, sternly.

"Okay, let me hear them," Dr. Hall nodded.

"What's today's date?"

"It's Wednesday. December 12th."

"Can I see the video of me again?"

"Sure," Dr. Hall said.

She opened her laptop and typed on her keyboard, then turned it towards Zoey and pressed the play icon on the video.

"Wait, pause it, please. I want to see what I'm wearing." Zoey leaned in closer to the screen. "Is that my... yeah... it is. That's my college T-Shirt," she said surprisingly, more so speaking to herself than to Dr. Hall. "I normally only wear that at home. Why would I have my purse with me?" Zoey squinted her eyes. "Wait, are my clothes wet? It was raining? Where are my clothes now? Why didn't I wake up wearing them?"

The questions came pouring out of her mouth uncontrollably.

"It did rain that night," Dr. Hall said. "Your clothes were soaked when the police brought you here, so we had you change into a hospital gown."

"You said today is Wednesday, so that means it was Monday night when I did this... that was the tenth then..." Zoey mumbled as her thoughts were all over the place.

"I know you have a lot of questions Zoey, but I think you should go get some breakfast and try to relax your mind. We can continue talking about this later during your session."

"No, I need to figure this out now," Zoey insisted.

"I have a phone conference in ten minutes. I'm sorry, I just don't have the time to start our session right now. Please go have some breakfast. I'll see you in the evening," Dr. Hall persisted.

"Fine!" Zoey groaned a lot louder than she expected to, then walked out of her office.

Feeling more aggravated than ever, she marched to the cafeteria, mumbling the whole way.

As soon as she walked in, Destiny who wore a hot pink T-shirt and tomato red leggings, waved her hand in the air from a table in the far corner. "Zo Zo, over here! I saved you a seat!"

Of course, you did.

Zoey awkwardly smiled and then went in line to get her breakfast, which was scrambled eggs, bacon, and greasy hash browns.

She slumped her way back towards Destiny's table, wishing that she would just be left alone.

"What took you so long to get here?" Destiny asked while she chomped on her bacon.

"I stopped at Dr. Hall's office. I had questions for her," Zoey sighed as she sat across from her.

"Ooooh! Like what?" Destiny's eyes beamed. She sure did love gossip.

"Nothing important," Zoey said, quickly.

"Well, it must've been if you went there, first thing this morning!" Destiny pressed.

Zoey swallowed a bite of her egg. "If you must know... I asked her what today's date is. She told me, then kicked me out of her office and now I'm here. End of story."

"You could've asked me that, silly," Destiny laughed. "You didn't have to go all the way to Dr. Hall, duh."

"I'll do that next time," Zoey smirked, then took a bite of her hash browns.

As she ate her food, the image of herself on video replayed in her mind and it made her cringe.

I can't believe I did that… there's just got to be a reasonable explanation for this. I'd never go to the cops! Unless I really had a reason to… my mom's not alive… that's ridiculous…

"Hello? Earth to Zoey?" Destiny snapped her fingers in front of Zoey's face.

"Huh? Oh sorry… were you saying something?" Zoey shook her head. "I zoned out. I'm just trying to remember how I got here."

"You'll figure it out. You probably can't remember because of the drugs they stuck you with when you first came in. It makes you forget everything," Destiny said.

Zoey thought back to the pain she felt in her arm on the first night she woke up.

"Oh yeah, that big guy… Tee or whatever his name is… he gave me some type of shot when I first woke up here."

"See what I mean, these ghouls are stab happy around here," Destiny widened her eyes and put her fork down, "especially Tee. Watch out for him!"

"I'll do that," Zoey sighed. She looked around the room at all the patients as she continued to take small bites of her food.

Kelsey was twitching in her seat. Derek sat across from her, shivering even though he wore a hoodie and sweatpants, while a few other patients sat at the other tables, silently eating.

I do not belong here…

Zoey turned her attention back to Destiny, who already ate all her food and was now standing up. She cupped her hands around her breasts. "Got to make sure they look perky!" she laughed and then pulled up her leggings, turning them into high waisted, rather than low.

"High waisted pants are better looking on me because of my high hips."

She looked over at the cafeteria nurse who sat quietly in the corner with a tablet in her hand and said loudly enough for her to hear, "someone should be taking notes! Now Zo Zo, it's been a blast, but I am off to find my future hubby!" She flipped her hair, then walked away from the table with her lunch tray, throwing the plate in the garbage can on her way out of the cafeteria.

I need to figure out how to get back home…

Zoey finished her food a few minutes later, then headed towards the nurse's station.

When she got there, Tee and two other nurses were sitting behind the glass in conversation. This time, she noticed the double doors on the other side, which according to Destiny was the entrance. She looked at them, contemplating whether to try to escape but decided against it as she knew in her better conscious, that attempting to run would probably only make things worse. Instead, she tapped impatiently on the glass.

"Can I have my purse?" she asked.

Tee got up from his chair, went in through a door in the back of the station, then came back out just a minute later with a big plastic bag in his hand. He walked out of the door connected to the hallway where Zoey stood and handed it to her.

The bag contained her purse and the now dry clothes she wore in the video. She pulled out her purse and opened it but noticed things were missing. She only saw her hairbrush, loose change, and a handful of receipts that she had been meaning to throw out.

"Where's my wallet, or my keys and my cell phone?"

"We have them. You'll get it back when you leave," Tee said.

"If I ever leave," Zoey muttered.

"That all depends on you," Tee shrugged.

Zoey rolled her eyes. "Can I take the rest of this stuff back to my room?"

Tee nodded, then walked back through the door to the nurse's station.

Even the staff is strange here.

Zoey headed back towards her room with the plastic bag. She turned down the hallway where Lisa and Tina's rooms were and spotted an elderly woman standing by herself. She looked completely lost, so Zoey thought to ask if she needed help. "Excuse me, ma'am, can I help—"

"No!" the old lady snapped, "and DO NOT call me ma'am. What's your name, kid?"

Her voice resembled the tone of a person who smoked cigarettes their entire life.

"It's uh… Zoey… What's yours?"

"Miriam. When did you get here kid?" She looked Zoey up and down.

I should've just kept walking.

"Yesterday… and I'm not a kid. I'm 25."

"Ya a kid in my eyes, kid!" Miriam said, hastily.

Why is this old woman a patient here?

"Miriam, if you don't mind me asking, why are you in here?"

"Because of my trashy sister," Miriam huffed. "I couldn't stand living with her, so I tried to die! And I wish I succeeded! This place sucks, kid. The world sucks. I tell ya… you don't want to get this old, Zoey. Ya get old and then the next thing ya know, everyone wants ya money!" Miriam shook her head angrily as she spoke. "Even if I did get out of here, I got nothing… the world sucks… we're all better off dead."

This poor woman…

"Wow, I'm sorry to hear that, Miriam," Zoey said softly.

"No, you're not. Ya know, I like you. You're young lookin', you're fresh. You don't belong here," Miriam shook her head.

"I agree with you," Zoey sighed.

"Now get out of my way kid. I'm going to go take a nap," Miriam said as she walked into the room next to her.

Okay, I can't end up like Miriam…

Instead of continuing towards her room, Zoey turned back around to go to the hallway phone. But when she got there, Derek was already using it.

Great… just what I need.

"How much longer are you going to be?" Zoey asked him.

Instead of answering, he glared sharply, then turned his back towards her.

44

"Uh, excuse me? I'm talking to you!" She tapped on his shoulder.

Derek immediately yelled, "don't touch me!" and dropped the phone, then darted down the hallway.

That was easier than I thought it would be.

Zoey picked up the phone that was now dangling from its cord.

"Hi, he'll call you back," she said to whoever he was speaking to and hung up.

She dialed Alex's number and after just two rings, she answered.

"Sis! It's me! Did you get my voicemail?!" Zoey cried out.

She was so excited to hear Alex's voice that she nearly screamed.

"I did! I tried to call the number back last night, but someone told me you were sleeping," Alex said.

"Who said that?"

"I don't know, it was a girl... she sounded really friendly. Why?"

"Hmm, I wonder if it was Destiny. I don't imagine anyone else answering this phone," Zoey said.

"Who... who is Destiny?" Alex asked, clearly confused.

"A girl that's locked up in here like me. Apparently, she has been in here since grandma died."

"Oh, uh okay... anyway, what happened?" Alex asked, wearily.

"I'm guessing you haven't seen it yet," Zoey groaned.

"Seen what? What are you talking about?"

"Go on my timeline. I'm sure someone's tagged me in it already. Although, I hope not..." Zoey rolled her eyes as she thought about it.

"Okay, I'm confused. Hold on, let me put you on speaker... okay, I'm on my newsfeed. So, what exactly am I looking... wait, is that you?!" Alex's voice became so loud; Zoey had to pull the phone away from her ear.

"What the... what happened? Are you okay? You thought your mom was alive? Why were you in front of the police station? Who took this?"

"Yeah, yeah, I'm fine right now," Zoey had to cut Alex off before she kept asking questions. "I'm just as confused as you are. I honestly, don't know what happened. I can't remember anything I did on Monday except for when I woke up in the morning but that's it. Then, I woke up here yesterday morning... and then this doctor showed me that video... I really honestly have never felt so confused in my whole life. When I first saw the video, I thought someone drugged me or I was drunk, but the doctor says I wasn't. They took my blood when they brought me here... which I don't remember them doing... and apparently, there was alcohol in my system but not enough to make me act that way. I don't even remember drinking though! Did I talk to you at all on Monday?"

"Monday... Monday," Alex paused, "well I know we didn't see each other because I was at work all day. I don't remember if we talked on the phone. Hold on, I'm checking my call logs right now… uh, no, we didn't talk but we did the day before. Oh yeah, I remember now. I called you in the morning before I went to work."

Zoey pulled out her notebook and pen and put them up against the wall.

"Okay, so the last time we spoke was on Sunday in the morning," she concluded as she jotted down a note. "Do you remember what we talked about? Did I say what I had planned on Monday?"

"You told me that you had a lot of editing to do and had some photoshoots coming up, but I don't remember if you said anything specifically about Monday," Alex said.

Zoey sighed, "alright… thanks."

"So, you're not allowed out of there at all? I can't even check you out!?" Alex sounded not only confused but aggravated that she couldn't help Zoey.

"Nope. According to the doctor, I was acting dangerous or whatever… and the cops didn't want to send me home alone like that, so they sent me here… I just don't get it. If they asked me to call someone, then why wouldn't I have called you? I don't remember anything. This is so strange…I'm… I'm kind of scared, to be honest," Zoey admitted.

"I bet you are. I'm confused too," Alex sighed, "but we'll figure it out and get you out of there. When can I visit you?"

"Oh, good question. Let me find out, hold on."

Zoey spotted a nurse a few feet away from her in the hallway and called out to ask her what time visiting hours were. She turned back towards the phone. "The nurse said between 9:00 to 10:00 a.m. and 8:00 to 9:00 p.m."

"Okay, well I'll come by tonight after work," Alex paused, "just try to stay calm... They can't make you stay there forever. I'm sure you'll remember what happened soon and they'll let you leave... there has got to be a reasonable explanation for this. You don't' belong there, sis."

"Ugh, who knows," Zoey groaned, "can you stop by my place and get my planner? They're keeping my phone. I hope that I wrote out my day... It wasn't in my purse so it must be on my desk or near it somewhere."

"Yeah, no problem. I'll see you, tonight."

Alex assured Zoey that everything would be okay and that she didn't belong in the hospital before saying goodbye. Then Zoey went back to her room, taking the plastic bag containing her purse and clothes with her.

I just need to make Dr. Hall understand that I'm not dangerous... and that I don't belong here...

She shoved the bag containing her belongings in the nightstand drawer when she got to her room then went into the bathroom. She stood in front of the sink and ran cold water on her face. She lifted her head and stared at herself through the mirror as water dripped off her cheeks and nose. The image of herself on video replayed in her mind and she shook her head.

"Why did I do that?" she asked herself out loud. She caught attention to her still very tangled hair, so she walked out of the bathroom and got her brush out of her purse.

Zoey sat at the edge of the bed and began to brush her hair. The pain from pulling at the knots started to irritate her and the more she became irritated, the more she brushed forcefully. A sudden burst of anger ran through her and she propelled the brush across the room. It smacked against the wall, bounced off the nightstand, then onto the floor.

"What is wrong with me?" Zoey sobbed as she watched her hands shake.

She got off the bed, picked the brush up, and put it into the nightstand drawer while trying to calm herself down.

I can't sit here alone... I need to distract myself...

Zoey went to walk out of her room, but Tee opened her door just as she was about to turn the doorknob.

"Uh, thanks for knocking... I could've been naked in here!" she huffed.

"I would suggest getting naked in the bathroom instead," he said in his monotoned voice.

It was ridiculously hard to tell when he was being sarcastic or serious.

"Duly noted," she mumbled.

"I heard a noise. Are you okay?" he asked as he glanced around the room.

"Does it look like I'm okay?" she scoffed, "You have me trapped here."

He poked his head in the bathroom, then stood back at the doorway and inspected the small room with his eyes once more.

"Let me know if you need anything," he said, then walked out, leaving the door open.

"Thanks for closing it!" Zoey yelled and marched angrily over to her bed.

She laid face down on her stomach as the rage inside her quickly turned into uncontrollable tears.

Half an hour later, Zoey ended up crying herself right to sleep.

4:30 P.M.

Zoey woke up half an hour before her scheduled session time. She quickly tied her hair into a high bun and headed out to Dr. Hall's office, hoping to hear good news.

I can get myself out of here… I can do this… this is just a misunderstanding.

Dr. Hall greeted her at the door just a few seconds after she knocked.

"Hello, Zoey come on in," she smiled.

Because I have another choice.

Zoey sat down in the chair and pulled out her notebook from her pocket.

After a moment of looking over the notes, the only thing Dr. Hall asked Zoey was about the book she could remember reading. "It's some mystery book. I forget the author. I just started it," Zoey shrugged.

"What is the mystery about?"

"I'm only on the third chapter, something about a love triangle gone wrong, where someone ends up dying. So, anyway," Zoey said, trying to move the conversation along.

"Anyway, so you told me your mother passed away but what about your father? Can you tell me about him?" Dr. Hall asked.

Zoey hesitated, "uh, my dad is my dad. There is nothing really to say. I see him occasionally."

"Do you two have a good relationship?"

"I guess... well, we did. I don't know. We only talk on the phone sometimes... There's nothing really to say anymore."

"What do you mean?" Dr. Hall continued questioning Zoey as she began typing on her laptop.

"I really don't want to talk about this..." Zoey said, uncomfortably.

"I'm not forcing you. I'm just trying to help you." Dr. Hall kept her calm tone, which was making Zoey more aggravated.

"Okay, but I don't think talking about my dad will tell me why I was screaming for my mom. I'm an adult and I was caught on camera running into a police station looking for Mommy," she shook her head, "I-I-I just... I don't get it."

"Why do you think you were looking for her, Zoey?" Dr. Hall asked.

Zoey took a deep breath. "I don't know. I don't know why I'm here... I just want to go home." Tears suddenly broke through her eyes. "Now I'm crying. Why, why, why is this happening to me?" Zoey stuttered as she started to hyperventilate.

"Deep breaths, Zoey. In and out. Do it with me. Breathe in," Dr. Hall said. She sat up straight in her chair and inhaled deeply. "Breathe out... in... and out..."

They both took several deep breaths until Zoey started to calm down.

"Do you normally get panic attacks?" Dr. Hall asked.

"No," Zoey exhaled, "well yeah, I did before... but I haven't got a really bad one in over a year. Not until just now... but what does that matter? Everyone my age gets them nowadays."

"Right," Dr. Hall agreed. "I even get them."

"You do?" Zoey asked, skeptically.

"Yes, I don't get them very often but there are times when life challenges me and I can get overwhelmed. There is nothing wrong with that. What is important is recognizing when you feel overwhelmed and how to handle it in that moment. You are more than your emotions. I like to remind myself that when times are tough, I just need to take a step back and breathe. Everything will always be okay in the end."

"I guess," Zoey slumped down in her chair feeling more defeated than ever.

"I guess if you want to know about my mom," she paused, "she was diagnosed with cancer when I was three years old. She had it for four years and then it went into remission for a year. Then it came back and then she had it for two years straight... before it killed her," she said morbidly.

Dr. Hall nodded, "I'm so sorry to hear that."

"Yeah... anyway," Zoey paused as she noticed Dr. Hall typing fiercely away and she tried leaning over the desk to see what was on the screen.

"I'm just making some notes in your chart," Dr. Hall said, closing the laptop. "You didn't go to activity time today. Why not?"

"Because I was sleeping… no one woke me up for it," Zoey sighed.

"It's okay to get some rest but I strongly suggest that you utilize activity time, Zoey. You decide to attend or not but if you would like to understand why you're here, I suggest that you follow what's on your schedule," Dr. Hall raised an eyebrow but still kept her kind tone as she spoke. "I think we can wrap up today and continue tomorrow."

"So, I'm stuck here for another night? Seriously?" Zoey asked in disbelief.

"You'll be okay Zoey," Dr. Hall smiled.

"Remember, you can call a nurse at any time you need."

"How kind," Zoey muttered. She left Dr. Hall's office and ran back to her room.

8:00 P.M.

"Hello, I came to visit my sister, Zoey Martin. She's in the psych ward part of the hospital," Alex said as she placed her license on the security desk.

The security guard leaned casually back in his chair and stared at her.

"Can you tell me which room she's in?" Alex demanded, hands on her hips.

The security guard sighed and typed on his computer keyboard. He grabbed her license and scanned it.

"Smile," he said while he held up a small camera.

"What are—" A flash from the camera stopped Alex from speaking, nearly blinding her.

The guard printed an ID sticker with her photo. It showed half of her forehead cut off and her mouth wide open.

"The normal entrance is closed at this time, so you have to go around." He pointed behind him. "Go through this hall to the end, take a left, then a right, then through the double doors to the end. The behavioral section is right outside of them."

He handed her license back, then called out to the person in line behind her.

Alex took her ID back and went to walk down the long hallway. She passed by numerous photos of surgeons, doctors, and nurses before making it to the end of the hallway. She took a left down another one then a right down another and after a few minutes, she reached the end but didn't see any double doors.

"Can I help you find something, honey?" a nurse passing by, asked Alex.

"Yes... I'm looking for the psych ward part of the hospital," Alex answered as she clearly looked confused.

The nurse's eyes widened. "Oh okay... It's behind you. Keep going down this hallway and take the first left. You'll see signs that will direct you from there."

Alex thanked her and rushed down the hall, through the lobby, and eventually found the double doors.

She walked through them and entered a room with another door. She rang the bell next to it, which prompted a buzzing noise. A second later, the door opened automatically, and she walked in just as a security guard, stood up.

"Empty your pockets of anything sharp and metal. Put your cell phone and purse in the locker. Then give me the key," he said.

Alex put her purse in one of the lockers except for Zoey's planner.

"Can I bring this to my sister?" she asked.

The security told her to put it on the belt and he picked it up and shook it for a moment before deeming it was okay. She walked forward and he hit a button on the elevator which made the doors open a second later. Alex walked in and he pushed the second-floor button from inside but did not go in with her.

"Have fun," he muttered just before the elevator doors shut.

The elevator went up one floor and the doors opened, showing a small door in front of it. She pressed the button next to it and waited until she heard a loud buzz. A moment later the door opened, and Tee was standing there.

"I'm here to see Zoey..." Alex said cautiously, as she looked behind him.

"This way," Tee said. He turned around and Alex followed him.

While walking, they passed two patients dancing in the hallway. One patient tried to grab Alex by the hand to dance but Tee intervened.

"Take a seat over there. I'll tell her you're here," he said as they walked into the activity room.

Alex sat in one of the chairs at the table. She noticed two patients laughing at the cartoons on T.V. and realized that Zoey definitely didn't belong.

"SIS!!!!" She heard Zoey call out from the doorway.

Alex jumped up from her seat. "Are you okay? Did they hurt you? Do I need to hurt someone?!"

"Relax, I'm fine. I'm just really happy to see you." Zoey smiled.

They went to sit back down at the table and Alex turned her back towards the door. She hunched over and put a hand up her shirt, then pulled out Zoey's planner. "I had to smuggle it in."

"Are you serious?!" Zoey asked, shocked.

Alex laughed, "No. I'm just kidding. I asked if I could bring it… just trying to make you laugh."

"You're funny," Zoey chuckled.

"What's funny, was me trying to find this place! First, the security guard sucks. No manners and no direction. I got lost for a whole fifteen minutes just in the hospital, so I had to ask a nurse where the psych ward was."

Zoey busted out laughing. "You probably made people think you're crazy like me."

"I don't care as long as I got here, right?" Alex shrugged.

Alex had always been a go-getter. She was a kind but stern person and when she needed to get something done or get somewhere, she made sure it happened.

"What's so funny, Zo Zo?" Destiny asked as she walked in the room, interrupting their laughter.

"Oh, nothing. Just my sister being my sister," Zoey grinned. "This is Alex. Alex, this is Destiny."

Destiny extended her arm out. "Nice to meet you."

"Nice to meet you too," Alex shook her hand.

"I'll let you two hang out Zo Zo," Destiny smiled and skipped back out of the room.

"Wow, I thought she was going to stay here and bother us," Zoey said in a whisper. "She's kind of clingy."

"Why are you whispering? She's gone..." Alex looked around, confused.

"You just never know what that girl can hear." Zoey said in a low tone while looking suspiciously at the door which made them both laugh again.

"Oh my god... I haven't laughed since yesterday or the day before or," she paused, "actually I don't even know when. Anyways, let's look through my planner. Maybe it will tell me something..."

She turned to the date of December 10th. It read:

9:00 – 11:00 a.m. do a workout at home or go for a mile run, spend 20 minutes reading and work on a few photos.
1:00 p.m. Christmas shoot.

"So why can't I remember anything after waking up that morning?" Zoey asked herself. She looked up from her planner to Alex. "There was nothing weird about my apartment or anything?"

Alex shook her head. "No. Everything seemed normal. I didn't notice anything anyway... But maybe I should go back and check. I can ask your neighbors if they saw you."

Zoey tapped her chin with her index finger. "Yeah, good idea. I just don't want them to think I'm insane."

"Well, you're not and they don't need to know where you are anyways."

"Unless they've seen the viral video of me that's surfacing the internet..." Zoey groaned.

"Yeah, well that could be possible... but hey!" Alex's voice perked up in a clear attempt to brighten Zoey's mood, "don't worry we'll figure it out. I'll stop by in the morning before work tomorrow." She looked around the room.

"Unless I can break you out of here today..."

"I'd love for you to try," Zoey said, even though they both knew it wasn't possible.

For the remainder of the half-hour, Alex tried to distract Zoey by telling her a story about a customer who spent an hour demanding to return a dress that she bought over two months ago. It had helped take her mind off things for the time being until Tee came into the room and told them that the visiting hour was over.

Zoey walked with them to the nurse's station and hugged Alex goodbye, wishing that she could walk out of the hospital with her.

One more night… that's all I'm going to spend here…

She headed back to her room, telling herself to stay positive. As she passed the phone in the hallway, the thought to call her dad crossed her mind but she quickly decided against it.

Not until I remember what happened to me…

2:00 A.M.

"Mom! Don't leave! Please, I need you, mom please!"

"Zoey! Zoey! It's okay, you're okay!"

"No! No… Don't leave! Come back… come back! NOOOOO!!!!"

Zoey could feel her whole body shaking and it was hard to control.

"It's okay. Relax. You're okay…"

Just as she went to reach out towards her mom, Zoey woke up to see Debra standing over her. She was speaking in a calm tone, repeatedly telling Zoey that she was okay while Tee held a firm grip onto her hands.

"L—let me go please," Zoey stammered as she tried to catch her breath.

Tee lifted his hands and she huddled against the wall and pulled her knees up to her chest. She could feel her heart racing against them as she gasped for breath.

"You were dreaming," Debra said as she held out a small pill and a glass of water towards Zoey. "Here, please take this. It will help you get back to sleep."

Zoey exchanged a look from the pill to Debra. "It's just to put me to sleep right?"

"Yes, just to put you to sleep, that's all," Debra smiled.

She reluctantly put the pill in her mouth and took a sip of water, then handed the glass back to Debra.

"Try to go back to sleep. My shift is almost over but there will be another nurse on duty if you need anything," Debra reassured her before walking out of the room with Tee, who to Zoey's surprise, closed the door behind him.

As soon as they left, she spit the pill out into her hand, then shoved it in between the mattress and bedsheet, then laid back down and looked up to the white ceiling. "What is going on with me? I haven't dreamt about you in almost a year," she thought out loud. The vague image of reaching out to her mom in the darkness lingered in Zoey's mind and the tears began to fall. She ended up lying in bed for the rest of the night until she cried herself back to sleep.

CHAPTER 3

DEC 13th

7:00 A.M.

Zoey woke up with a stabbing headache that ran throughout her forehead. She figured it was the effect of all the crying and lack of sleep she got the night before. Her stomach started to rumble as soon as she sat up, so she decided to go straight to the cafeteria.

But before walking out of her room, she went to the bathroom to run cold water over her face and looked at herself in the mirror, disappointed in what she saw. Her normally pale skin was beginning to look even paler, and her eyes had dark circles around them. Her hair was so greasy from not washing it in days, that it looked wet.

I'm starting to look like I really do belong here.

She glanced over at the shower and shook her head.

"I'm getting out of here today. I can wait until I get home... it'll be fine," she told herself, then went to go get breakfast.

When she got to the cafeteria, there was only one other patient sitting at a table, eating their food. Zoey grabbed her plate of over-easy eggs and bacon, then sat down at one of the empty tables alone, happy to eat in peace. She never liked socializing with people when she ate.

However, just a few minutes after she sat down, Lisa walked in, got her breakfast and went straight to Zoey's table.

"Hey, Zoey!" She had a plate of eggs in one hand and a children's doll in the other.

There goes my peace and quiet.

"Have you met my baby? This is Sofia," Lisa said as she sat down.

"No, I haven't," Zoey groaned.

"She's hungry." Lisa held a forkful of eggs up to the doll's mouth. Then she took a bite from the fork herself.

"Lisa, do you happen to know why Destiny's in here?" Zoey asked curiously.

Lisa stopped feeding her doll and put her fork down.

"Oh, girl yes! Let me spill all the tea!" she said excitedly.

"Destiny's foster parents made her come here a while back. I think they were only taking care of her for like two months before it happened."

"Before what happened?" Zoey interrupted.

Lisa lowered her head and looked both left, then right before whispering, "she tried to jump out of the car when they were driving down the highway! Shh! Don't tell her I told you that, though!"

Okay, that's it... I need to get out of here today. I for sure did not try to kill myself. I am not an arsonist... and I'm not whatever Derek is... or Kelsey.

"Oh, wow," Zoey responded, not sure what to say. "So, how long has she been here, then?"

"Oh, she's been in and out of here A LOT!" Lisa said, dragging out her words, "I think she was like 16 years old when she first came here."

That's four years of being in and out of this place. I've been here only three days and I'm already on the verge of losing my mind.

"Hey ladies!" Zoey suddenly heard Destiny call out from the doorway.

She walked into the cafeteria and sat right next to her.

"What about your food Destiny?" Zoey asked. "Aren't you going to get in line?"

Then I can escape you.

"Nah, I'm not hungry this morning," Destiny shook her head. "The meds sometimes make me nauseous when I wake up." She stuck her tongue out, "bleh, I rather starve!"

"BASTARDS! IDIOTS! GET OUT OF MY WAY!" Miriam hissed as she walked into the cafeteria along with a few other patients. "Seniors first!"

"Oh, Miriam," Destiny sighed. "What a soulless witch."

"Idiots is her favorite word!" Lisa giggled, then covered her mouth as if she said something she wasn't supposed to.

"I met her yesterday. What's the deal with her sister?" Zoey asked.

"Oh, let me explain it," Lisa began, "Miriam was—"

"Ah, ah, ah," Destiny shook her finger in the air to shush Lisa. "I'll explain it."

She slid an inch closer to Zoey.

I shouldn't have asked...

"Okay so, Miriam was this fancy rich lady for like her whole entire life," Destiny explained. "That was up until her husband died. I think she was a CEO of some tech company. I don't know the name of it but anywho, her husband died from a heart attack thirty years ago, and then she retired right after. So then," Destiny spoke like she was narrating a movie, "she isolated herself from everyone for YEARS and no one knew where she was until—"

"Wait, how old is Miriam now?" Zoey interrupted.

"She's 80 years old. Anywho," Destiny batted her eyes, clearly irritated with Zoey's interrupting.

"As I was saying... a few years ago, Miriam's sister convinced her to allow her to move into her house to take care of her and I guess that soulless witch of a sister tried to control Miriam and all her money, which Miriam obviously didn't like. I mean, who would right? So eventually, Miriam couldn't take it anymore and she tried to kill herself a few months ago." Destiny took a sip of her juice before continuing.

"And that Zo Zo, is how she ended up here."

What did I just hear?

"Wow that's craz-" Zoey stopped herself from using the term crazy and instead finished her sentence with the word, "heavy."

None of these stories are like mine. All I did was look for my dead mother… and forget why I did it.

Zoey shook her head, trying to shake away the image of herself on video. She stood up with her tray. "Well, thanks for the story but I'm done eating. I'll see you later."

"Wait, where are you going?" Destiny asked while crossing her arms, which Zoey was starting to notice was a signature move of hers when she didn't like something.

Somewhere to be away from all of you.

"I didn't get much sleep last night, I'm going to go get some rest," Zoey tried to say in a tone where she didn't sound aggravated.

"Oh okay, rest up my dear," Destiny uncrossed her arms and stood up. "I have an early session anyway. Time to go get the life sucked out of me. Toodles, ladies!" She skipped past Zoey out of the cafeteria and Zoey went back to her room.

When she got there, she closed the door behind her, desperately wishing to lock it. She started to pace up and down, hands on her hips as she let her mind wander back to Monday.

"If I forgot a whole damn day, who's to say I won't forget anything else?" she thought out loud. "I need to remain calm. They can't keep me here forever." Frantic, Zoey pulled out her notebook and began writing.

DECEMBER 10TH - WHAT DID I DO ALL DAY?
9 a.m. - WAS SUPPOSED TO GO FOR A RUN / EXERCISE/ EDIT - BUT DID I?

1 p.m. - WAS SUPPOSED TO HAVE A PHOTOSHOOT - BUT DID I? WHO WAS MY CLIENT?
WHAT I KNOW FOR SURE:
I RAN INTO THE POLICE STATION LIKE AN INSANE WOMEN AND I WOKE UP IN A PSYCH WARD THE NEXT DAY.

I ran into the police station in the rain...
Zoey stopped writing and thought about the video, then suddenly remembered she had no shoes on. "That's why my feet were hurting..." she gasped as she thought about the mild pain in her feet the first night she woke up.

The pain had subsided, and Zoey had forgotten about it until now.

She set the notebook aside and pulled off her now very dirty white socks that the hospital provided to her on the first day. There were light bruises on the bottom of both her feet and her right foot had a small scratch on the heel.

"Why the hell would I go outside without shoes?" she asked herself.

Zoey's mind was full of questions. The amount of confusion she felt was becoming extremely hard to handle and she wanted answers but knew that no one was going to help her, except for herself.

Why is this happening to me?

She laid down on the small hospital bed, flat on her back and listened to the distant thunder outside of the hospital, dangling her feet off the bedside.

"I'm literally stuck here... how did I do this to myself?"

Her emotions were turning from straight confusion to agitation, and she could feel the bones in her body tingle. Now, all she wanted to do was throw something or punch a wall to alleviate the amount of anger building up inside of her. She was just about to scream when she felt a tear fall down her cheek and in a matter of seconds, her face became flooded with more. Once again, she was crying uncontrollably and her body was shaking, just as it had in Dr. Hall's office.

Not another panic attack. Not again.

Zoey sat up and started to do the breathing techniques that Dr. Hall taught her, but she was crying so hard that it seemed almost impossible to inhale properly.

Suddenly the door to her room opened, breaking Zoey out of her attack.

A nurse with a blonde bob and a big smile stood in the doorway. "Hi dear, I was passing by your room, and I thought I heard you in distress. Can I do anything to help? Would you like to talk?" she asked kindly. Unlike Tee, it was easy to see that this nurse actually enjoyed her job.

"I--I'm fine," Zoey sniffled through short breaths.

The nurse stepped into the room and stood at the foot of her bed.

"Have you tried deep breaths? Breathe in and out… in and out," she said.

Zoey stopped sniffling as her breathing started to normalize. "I'm okay, thank you," she said as she fixed her posture, wiping away the tears.

The nurse reminded her she was just down the hall, then walked out of the room.

Zoey laid back down, pulled the covers over her head, and attempted to fall asleep.

2:00 P.M.

When Tee knocked on Zoey's already opened door, she woke up feeling groggy. She wasn't sure what time she fell asleep, but she was sure that she needed more of it.

"It's activity time. Wake up," he said.

Zoey rolled over, slightly pulling the covers down from her eyes.

"Do you know how to knock before opening a door?"

"Yes, I do," he smirked.

"Then why don't you do that?" she groaned.

"Cause it's more fun this way," he shrugged, then walked away.

I hate this place... I hate this place...

Zoey reluctantly got out of bed and went to head towards the activity room.

On her way there, she stopped at the phone in the hallway to call Alex.

"Hey, it's me! Did you get a chance to stop by my apartment this morning?" she asked as soon as Alex answered.

"Yes, I did. I was about to call you. I stopped by your apartment around 7:00 this morning and I knocked on the old lady's door right next to yours."

"That's so early," Zoey laughed. "Did she answer the door with a shotgun?"

"Surprisingly not! But she was not happy that I knocked so early. Anyway, she told me that she saw you leave for work Monday around noon. She was sitting outside her door and asked you where you were going. She said that you told her that you were running really late for a photoshoot and you looked flustered."

"Flustered? And that was it? I just left after that?" Zoey paused. "I don't remember that. I wonder why I was running late."

"Me too. You're barely ever late to your shoots," Alex remarked. "You're always early..."

"Yeah, I know. Did she ask what was going on?"

"Nope. She just seemed annoyed by me. I probably shouldn't have knocked that early... Oh well, at least I got my answers," Alex said.

Zoey chuckled, "Alright, thanks. I'll let you go. I have to go socialize with the other crazies, now."

"Stay strong, you'll be out of there soon. I'm getting off work too late tonight, but I'll try to come by tomorrow. Hopefully I won't have to though... maybe you'll be allowed to leave today," Alex said, trying to sound hopeful.

"I really hope so. I don't know how much longer I can do this... I'll talk to you later."

They said goodbye and Zoey went to the activity room.

As soon as she walked in, she saw Dr. Hall and the other patients sitting in a circle on the floor.

"Come take a seat, Zoey," Dr. Hall invited her to sit in the open space next to her.

"What is this?" Zoey asked hesitantly.

"This is group circle. I like for all of us to sit down occasionally to discuss a few topics. Today, we are going to share how we are feeling, what makes us angry and why. We were just getting started," Dr. Hall said. She looked at Derek. "How are you doing? Do you have anything to share with us?"

"We're doing fine today... We feel happy," Derek said in a low tone.

Zoey tried to hide the mix of horror and confusion on her face.

Tina raised her hand. "What makes me angry is the fact that my sister and I are here and not out there," she said as she pointed to the window.

"I can understand how that can make you mad Tina, but you know as well as I do that you need to be mentally ready to be on your own. Do you think you are ready yet? Have you thought about what you would do once you do get out of here?" Dr. Hall asked.

Tina looked down at her lap and sighed, "not really."

Dr. Hall looked around the circle. "Has anyone here thought about what they would do outside of the hospital?"

"You mean in the real world?!" Derek gasped.

"We are in the real world stupid," Tina scoffed.

"So, let's talk about how we deal with anger," Dr. Hall continued. "Will, how about you go first?"

"Well, I used to play video games, but I can't do that here," Will said hastily.

70

"We color," Derek whispered.

"Freak," Destiny laughed.

"Be nice Destiny. Apologize to Derek," Dr. Hall scolded.

Destiny rolled her eyes. "I don't apologize to people. They apologize to me."

"Sofia helps me!" Lisa gleefully said as she tightly held onto her doll.

"Tina, how about you?" Dr. Hall asked.

"Uhm, exercise," Tina said as more of a question than an answer.

Zoey gathered that Tina probably didn't do anything to alleviate her anger at all. She didn't seem like a happy person, but yet she didn't seem as angry as Will, who was sinisterly staring ahead. His eyes were bloodshot from barely blinking.

"Zoey, how do you cope with feeling angry?" Dr. Hall asked.

Zoey didn't answer and instead just shrugged her shoulders.

Dr. Hall gave her an annoying smile, then continued talking.

"It's always good to try to shift your focus once you start getting those feelings of aggravation, irritation, and sadness. Things like exercise, meditating, video games; those are all good choices. We must take notice of these mood changes right when we start feeling them," Dr. Hall paused, "It's almost like a disease. If you get checked and find out that something is wrong early enough to be treated, there is a better chance of it going away, right? But if you wait too long to go to the Doctor, it could get worse and you have a higher chance of not getting it treated. It is the same with emotions. If we ignore our negative emotions, they linger. They stay longer and gradually get worse but if we accept them, instead of pushing them away, then we can turn them into positive emotions instead."

"Angry is all you feel when you reach my age!" Miriam huffed, who was sitting alone on the couch.

"Miriam, if you want to be a part of our discussion, you have to sit with us," Dr. Hall continued, "now what about when we're feeling sad?"

"We try to think of happy things like flowers and puppies," Derek, who was hugging his knees to his chest, volunteered.

Destiny and Tina busted out laughing at the same time and Lisa awkwardly started to join them, not sure of what she was laughing at.

"AHHHH!" Derek screamed, then ran out of the room, nearly tripping over his own feet. This time it was Zoey who joined them in laughing.

That was surprisingly funny.

Dr. Hall stood up. "Okay, let's end our circle early. Destiny, I would like to start our session sooner today. Please come to my office in half an hour."

"Yes, Dr. Grinch," Destiny said as she saluted her.

Dr. Hall told everyone to have a great day, then walked out of the room.

"You all make me sick!" Miriam suddenly yelled as she threw the controller at the wall, startling not only Zoey but most of the rest of the patients too.

I do not belong in this place...

5:00 P.M.

"How did you like group circle today?" Dr. Hall asked as she leaned back in her office chair.

"It was alright," Zoey paused, "although, I don't believe I should be in group therapy with people who refer to themselves as plural, like Derek does. I'm not crazy like him."

"Derek isn't crazy either," Dr. Hall smiled. "He has multiple personality disorder."

"Yeah. I figured," Zoey muttered. "Anyway, I have more notes I wrote down. Here,"

she said as she pulled out her notebook and set it on the desk.

"My sister brought me my planner last night... since you guys won't give me my phone."

"Okay good, this is a start. Does this help you recall any other part of your day?" Dr. Hall asked as she looked at what Zoey wrote.

"No, not really but something definitely had to happen because my neighbor said I was running late to my shoot... I'm rarely ever late. I always arrive at least fifteen minutes early to make sure I set up properly."

Dr. Hall pushed the notebook aside.

"Why didn't you eat lunch today, Zoey?" she asked, abruptly changing the subject.

"I was sleeping… no one woke me up for it… again," Zoey sighed. "It's important to eat all your meals, Zoey. Are you sustaining an appetite?" Dr. Hall asked.

This woman clearly has never eaten any of this food here.

Zoey stared blankly and nodded her head, yes.

"So, let's talk about your job. How long have you been a photographer? Do you enjoy it?"

"Yeah, it's alright," Zoey shrugged. "I've been in photography for two years now. It's actually my busiest time of the season right now. I get a lot of people that usually want holiday photoshoots of their families for Christmas and New Year's."

"Oh wow, that sounds so fun!" Dr. Hall said, enthusiastically.

"I guess if you call that fun…" Zoey rolled her eyes.

"Your notes said that you had a Christmas shoot on Monday. Was that for a family?" Dr. Hall asked.

"Well, I guess it would have to be… All my Christmas shoots are of families," Zoey paused as she thought about it. "Wait… I know how I can find out! I can't believe I didn't think of this before. I need to check my emails. There should be a confirmation email from whoever I was supposed to photograph that day. Can I use your computer?"

"Not mine," Dr. Hall shook her head. "You can use the computer in the activity room, but Debra has to monitor you."

"Fine with me," Zoey said and began to stand up, eagerly.

"Not so fast," Dr. Hall stopped her. "Sit back down."

"But I really think this will help me remember what I did," Zoey said impatiently.

"First of all, you can't access the computer without Debra and she's already gone for the night. Tomorrow, during regular activity hours, you can ask her to log on," Dr. Hall said.

Zoey sat back down and sighed.

"Second of all," she continued, "I would like to discuss your family again."

"How is talking about my family going to help me with why I'm here?" Zoey asked. Her anxiousness and aggravation were now growing by the minute and her legs were shaking in her seat.

Breathe, breathe…

"Well, you were concerned about your mom at the station. Has she been on your mind a little more than usual recently?"

"I guess," Zoey paused, "but that's only because it was her birthday last week."

"I see. How do you normally handle that day?"

"I treat it like any other day of my life… I just go about my day and try to make time to go to the cemetery… if I get there, I get there. If not, she understands."

Dr. Hall typed on her laptop for a few seconds before speaking again.

"So, we talked about getting a source of grieving therapy before and you said you never received any at all. How did you cope with your mother's death when it happened?"

I had no choice.

"I just got through it…" Zoey hesitated, "I don't know. I was a teenager. You get over stuff quickly at that age… it's not like I really got over her dying… I just, I don't know. Again, I was a teenager. I had a lot of friends to distract me at that time."

"So," Dr. Hall continued, "tell me about the rest of your family. What is your relationship like with them?"

"I have five uncles and one aunt. Two of my uncles live down the street from me and the other three live with my aunt in Texas… but I don't talk to any of them. I haven't since my mom died."

"Why is that?" Dr. Hall asked.

Zoey groaned. "I'm not really sure. They never called me after she died and I never called them," she paused, "but I was a teenager… they were the adults. I was just a kid. They should have called me. I'm the one who lost my mom. They got to have her in their life way longer than I did."

Wow, I have never actually said that out loud…

Zoey could hear the aggravation in her own words as she spoke, and it shocked her.

"And that seems to frustrate you," Dr. Hall concluded.

How observant of you.

"I guess," Zoey rolled her eyes, growing more irritated.

"So, after Leanne passed away, it was just you and your dad?" Dr. Hall asked. "Why did you move out so soon?"

She moves through these subjects fast.

"I was a stupid teenager, that's probably why," Zoey grimaced.

All these questions about her family were aggravating her more than ever.

"Everyone has their own way of grieving. There is no right or wrong way Zoey. Maybe that was your way of grieving, you wanted to be independent," Dr. Hall suggested.

Zoey shifted in her seat. "I guess, I just wanted to feel more in control of my life. I didn't have much of a childhood honestly... all I can really remember about it is going to different hospitals since my mom was constantly sick."

"Zoey, I think the first step you need to take is controlling your anxiety," Dr. Hall said.

How did she get anxiety from all of that?

"Um, it's not that bad," Zoey argued, "I told you I haven't had a panic attack like I did the other day in a long time, I swear."

"No, but I think it's somewhere to start. You're feeling anxious right now. Look at your legs," Dr. Hall said.

She raised her eyebrows as she nodded towards Zoey's rapidly shaking legs.

"I'm going to prescribe you a medication. You can start by taking it once a day with your food, either in the morning or at dinner. It's just to control your anxiety for right now and help with your panic attacks," she said.

Now I'm getting put on medication... this is not progress.

"Also, why don't you stop at the nurse's station and ask for a hospital gown or some new clothes, Zoey. I think it's time that you've changed out of the ones you are in."

Zoey looked herself up and down and realized that she'd been wearing the same pair of baggy sweats and T-shirt for the past three days.

I should probably shower too...

Instead of arguing about the medication, which Zoey so desperately wanted to do, she nodded to everything else Dr. Hall said and they ended their session shortly after. She left her office and went straight to the nurse's station which the nurse behind the glass was happy to look for something for Zoey when she asked for new clothes. A few minutes later, she came back with a pair of sweatpants and a hospital gown.

"This is all we have clean right now..." the nurse said and half-smiled. "I'm sorry... you can always borrow from other patients too."

Are you kidding me?

"Uh, thanks..." Zoey had no energy to fight, so she took the clothes and went back to her room.

She took a very quick shower when she got there but opted out in washing her hair as she didn't want to spend extra time alone without the door locked. She got out and changed into the sweatpants and hospital gown, which reached her ankles, so she tied it up at her waist to make it fit like a shirt.

Zoey looked at herself in front of the mirror of the bathroom in disbelief.

"This is really happening to me... I look a mess."

She shook her head, then went to lay in bed.

Her thoughts jumped everywhere from wondering why she told the police her mother was alive to how she was going to get herself out of the hospital.

"Mom... if you're listening... please... please help me. Why can't I remember anything? What happened to me?"

Zoey closed her eyes and eventually cried herself to sleep hours later.

CHAPTER 4

DEC 14th

8:30 A.M.

"Mom! Hey! Wait! Wait! I see you! Stop! Wait for me!"

The music, the lights and the amount of people all blurred together.

"I knew it was you! Stay there! I'm coming!"

Zoey rushed through the rain as it fell hard, making it difficult for her to see ahead.

"I'm here! Wait, wait for me..."

Lightning suddenly struck followed by the sound of a loud thud.

"Oh my god!" Zoey woke up instantly from both the sound of thunder outside of the hospital and the thud of Tee's knuckles knocking against the door.

Now he learns to knock.

"Wake up," he said as he swung the door open. "There's only an hour left for breakfast if you want it."

"I'm up," Zoey sighed as she sat upright in bed.

Tee nodded and walked away, leaving her door open.

What the hell was I just dreaming?

Feeling lethargic, Zoey grabbed her notebook from the nightstand, turned to a new page, and wrote:

12/14 – Dreamt that I saw mom somewhere. I couldn't get to her, there were a lot of people, I think it was raining.

Zoey could barely remember what happened since Tee distracted her by knocking and now, she felt irritated. Her stomach started to rumble, which reminded her that she hadn't eaten lunch or dinner the day before.

Breakfast is probably getting cold by now... I'll starve it out until lunch...

She got up to close her door, hoping that Tee would not come back to open it. Then she sat back down and read through all her notes again.

This is too much... I can't do this...

A weight felt like it had fallen on her chest and she could not get it off. She gazed around the room and became completely lost in where she was. The walls seemed smaller and her breathing became difficult.

"Deep, deep breaths..." Zoey tried to remind herself to breathe, but her impatience started to take over, and she began crying.

The fact that Zoey was crying made her angrier. Her arms and legs now tingled, along with her head which throbbed, terribly. She started to count out loud in between deep breaths, while holding tightly on to the edge of the bed, rocking her body back and forth.

Control my breathing. In through my nose, out through my mouth...

After a few inhales and exhales, Zoey started to calm down. Suddenly, she remembered her session with Dr. Hall the night before and her mood instantly lightened. She leaped up from her bed.

My emails! I need to check my email!

"NOOOOOOO!" someone shouted out from the hallway.

What the hell is going on now?

She walked over to her door and peeked out the window just in time to see two nurses run by in a hurry.

What the...

Zoey opened the door and poked her head out towards the direction of which they ran.

Tee and another guard were holding Derek onto the floor in front of his room. One of the nurses held his head in place as he tried to squirm out of her grip, while the other nurse was approaching him with a needle the size of a horse tranquilizer.

Oh, I can't watch this...

Just as Zoey went to look away, the nurse stuck the needle in Derek's arm.

A moment later, he stopped squirming and his body became limp.

Oh my god... did they just put him to sleep?!

Tee, the other guard and nurse let go and helped him to his feet. The guard and nurses walked away, leaving Tee to carry Derek into his room.

Zoey slowly closed her door and crawled back into her bed, shocked at what she just saw.

I need to get myself out of this place, today.

12:00 P.M.

As soon as the clock hit noon, Zoey was the first one standing in line for lunch. She managed to eat quickly enough before anyone could come in and bother her. When she finished eating and began heading out the door, the cafeteria nurse stopped her.

"Would you like your medicine this morning?" she asked as she held out a small white pill towards Zoey.

I forgot about this crap...

Zoey hesitated for a moment, then took the pill and put it in her mouth, acting as if she swallowed. To her surprise, the nurse nodded and walked away, seemingly unsuspicious.

Zoey held it in her mouth until she reached the end of the hallway and nonchalantly acted like she coughed but spit the pill into her hand. She then slickly hid it in the pocket of her sweatpants, as she looked around cautiously to see if anyone was watching. She knew that if she went back to her room, she would end up getting angry as she was too impatient to check her emails so, for the following hour she walked around the hallways just to kill the time.

It was just ten minutes until 2:00 p.m. when she walked into the activity room, where she saw Debra helping another patient color.

"Excuse me, Dr. Hall told me that you can help me get on the computer. I need to check my email," Zoey tried to ask in a calm tone.

"Oh, sure," Debra smiled and walked over to the computer.

Zoey followed her and Debra logged on, then pulled out the chair next to her and sat down in it. "I'll just be sitting right here."

Right… because no one's allowed any real privacy around here…

Zoey logged into her email account and scrolled by several unread emails from within the last few days until she reached one that had already been opened. The subject read: **Photoshoot Davis Confirmation Dec 10th 1:00 p.m.**

She clicked on the email feeling hopeful. It read:

Hello Sir, I am just confirming for your photoshoot this coming Monday at 1:00 p.m. I will arrive about 15 to 30 minutes prior so I can have enough time for proper set up. Let me know if you have any questions. Looking forward to it!

Davis… Davis family. Zoey could not put a face to the name. There was no photo on his email avatar, but his phone number and address were in a previous email.

Just as she started to wonder if it would be a good idea to call him, Lisa walked over and distracted her.

"Can I use the computer, Miss Debra?" she asked.

"Yes, when Zoey gets done," Debra said. "I'm sorry Zoey, but I'll give you about five more minutes, okay? We have to share here."

"That's fine," Zoey mumbled. She wrote down Mr. Davis's number in her notebook, then clicked off her email and logged into her social media hoping that she posted a video, picture, or just something that would help her remember anything from Monday.

"Are you done yet?" Lisa interrupted again.

"Just two more minutes, Lisa," Zoey hissed as she scrolled through her profile.

Her most recent activity was on December 8th. She posted a Christmas photo of a family that she photographed weeks prior but didn't see anything posted on December 10th. She typed the name *Davis* in the search bar, hoping to see an account that would look vaguely familiar but unfortunately, after looking through several, Zoey could not recognize any of them. She refreshed her newsfeed once more before deciding to log off and instantly regretted it.

It didn't take more than a few scrolls until the horrendous video of Zoey popped up on her feed. Someone that she never met before reposted it from someone else, who had reposted it from another person.

I can't believe this is happening.

"Okay Zoey, it's Lisa's turn," Debra said.

"All yours," Zoey sighed as she logged off.

She walked over to the phone and dialed Alex's number. After a few rings, she answered, and Zoey quickly began rambling. She wasn't sure if she should call her client or not, so she decided to ask Alex. Her mind felt like it was on fire and it was becoming hard to think straight.

"I think I should call him to find out if I went to his house… I can't remember anything past waking up so I need to figure out if I at least went there or not… this is the only thing I can think of," Zoey sighed.

"It's a good idea but… be prepared for what he might say," Alex said. "What if you didn't show up and he's mad about it or," she paused, "what if something really bad happened on the photoshoot? Then, what are you going to say?"

She's right… What am I going to say? Calling a client from a psych ward is probably not the best for business.

Zoey groaned, "yeah… you're actually right-"

"Zo Zo!" Destiny called out from the other side of the room, distracting Zoey from what she was about to say.

"Come look at my art!" Destiny held up a piece of paper that showed a drawing of a dark red heart surrounded by gray smoke and orange fire.

"A replica of the fire inside of us," she said dramatically.

"I'm going to set the outside of you all on fire if you don't shut the hell up!" Miriam scoffed from the couch, "I'm trying to watch a movie ya nim wits."

Destiny gasped loudly, "Nurse Debra! That hag just threatened me!"

"Miriam please," Debra warned.

Miriam huffed and began to raise the volume of the television.

"Miriam do not raise that any louder please," Debra said sternly.

Miriam however, didn't listen and turned it to its maximum volume.

Now, the usual ditzy smile on Debra's face dropped as she got up from her chair. This was the first time that Zoey saw Debra look even remotely mad. She watched her walk over to Miriam, grab the remote out of her hand, and turn off the television.

"There, now none of you get to watch anything. You can thank Miriam for that," she said to the two other patients that were sitting on the couch.

"Idiots!" Miriam scoffed, then walked out of the room.

"There she goes back to hide in her cave," Destiny laughed.

"That's enough Destiny," Debra scolded.

Destiny pushed herself back from the desk, nearly knocking it over. "Ugh, whatever. I'm done anyway."

Don't come over here, don't come over here...

"That Witch needs to crawl back into her cave with the rest of her bats!" Destiny huffed as she marched over to Zoey.

Of course, you're going to come over here.

"What the heck is going on over there? Are you okay?" Alex was asking repeatedly through the phone.

Zoey was so distracted by Miriam and Destiny that she forgot she was still on the phone.

"Oh yeah, I'm fine. Uh, I'll call you back," she said and hung up before Alex could say anything else.

"Stupid old people," Destiny pouted. She dropped to the floor and sat under the phone. "My grandma was never that stupid."

"What was your grandma like?" Zoey asked and sat down next to her.

Destiny pulled her knees to her chest and rested her chin on top of them. Her usual confident tone became almost as childlike as Lisa always sounded.

"She was the best grandma ever! We would sing Christmas songs together while she played the piano. I wish there was a piano here. Christmas is boring now... especially here."

Crap... Christmas is in a few days...

It wasn't until Destiny mentioned Christmas, that Zoey realized how close it was. Although the holidays often made her sad as she normally spent them alone, Zoey knew she didn't want to spend them in the hospital.

"Hopefully, I'll be out of here by Christmas," she said, hoping that saying the words out loud would make them come true.

"Good luck," Destiny sighed as she stood up.

She straightened her posture and wiped away her non-existent tears.

"Anywho my Zo Zo, no time for tears. Tears make you ugly."

She walked over to the window and gazed out at the courtyard. "I can't wait until the weather gets better so we can finally go outside."

"I didn't know we could go outside," Zoey said.

"Oh yeah, we're allowed during activity time once in a while when Dr. Grinch says so, but since the weather has been stupid, we can't."

Maybe I can escape that way…

Zoey looked out the window at the small courtyard protected by barbed wire. There wasn't a gate and the only way into the yard was from inside the hospital. She would have to climb the near ten-foot fence and somehow not get cut from the wire.

"I need to get out of here," she groaned.

"Girl, good luck. This place is like a prison," Destiny laughed.

"I've noticed," Zoey sighed.

"So, you really don't know how you got here yet?" Destiny asked.

"Not the slightest," Zoey shook her head.

"You don't remember looking for your mom? It was on video; how do you not remember?" Destiny questioned.

Zoey looked at Destiny confused. "How do you know about the video?"

"I told you, I know everything here… duh! It's fine. Don't be embarrassed. I tried jumping out of a car before," Destiny chuckled, "which obviously didn't work."

"Yeah, I kind of heard..." Zoey said cautiously as she remembered Lisa begging her not to tell Destiny.

"Lisa, I bet? She's such a chatty Cathy!" Destiny shook her head. "It's fine. Don't worry, I won't tell her." She sat on the floor again and pulled her knees to her chest. "Ugh, I miss my grandma."

Zoey sat down next to her and pulled her knees up to her chest too. "I miss my mom."

"What happened to her, Zo Zo?"

"She died from cancer ten years ago."

"My grandma died five years ago," Destiny paused, "she was old though." She looked down at her pink socks. "My mom died too... and my dad. They both got killed in a car crash together when I was five. I don't remember them very much, though. Do you remember your mom?"

"Mm, yes and no... it's complicated. I mean, I knew my mom a lot longer than you got to know your parents but as I'm getting older, I forget things about her..." Zoey's voice trailed off as she realized this was the first time speaking about forgetting her childhood memories with someone.

"Like what?" Destiny asked.

"Like just things we did together," Zoey said as she stretched her feet out. She leaned her head back against the wall. "There was this one time when we went to Disney world, but I don't remember what it really looked like. When I think back to it, I just remember wearing a Disney sweatshirt with mouse ears on my head, walking around the park next to my dad. He was pushing my mom in a wheelchair... I still don't even know why she was in a wheelchair. That's the only time I can recall her being in one."

"I've never been to Disney," Destiny pouted.

"Wish I could tell you how it was," Zoey said, dryly.

They both looked at each other and softly laughed.

Destiny rested her head on Zoey's arm. "Maybe you really did see your mom," she said.

That's doubtful.

"I don't know what I saw. I don't think I know who I am anymore..." Zoey sighed. "Destiny, why did you try to jump out of the car?"

Zoey suddenly felt a tear drop down her arm.

"Because when grandma died, those vampires took me in and I just didn't belong with them," Destiny said through sniffles. "They didn't get me. The man was nice, but the woman wasn't... but of course, nobody would believe me."

"I'm sorry, Destiny," Zoey sighed.

"I'm sorry too, Zo Zo."

5:00 P.M.

Zoey sat in Dr. Hall's office across from her in the same uncomfortable wood chair for the fourth time this week.

"So, I had a dream last night or... this morning. I'm not really sure..." she started to explain. "In the dream, I was looking for my mom and I guess I spotted her. I kept calling her name but every time I did, I never got to her... she just kept disappearing. There were a lot of lights and people, I don't know..." Zoey sighed.

She stopped talking as she didn't think what she was saying made any sense.

"Have you ever had a dream like that before?" Dr. Hall asked.

"Not really... I've only had a few dreams about her but nothing like that..."

"Did you write that down in your notes?"

"Yeah, I've been trying to write down everything."

"That's good. I want you to keep writing everything down. Maybe that is a good anxiety relief technique for you? Writing... that is not far off from photography. It's two ways to express your feelings," Dr. Hall suggested.

"I guess you're right," Zoey said softly.

Dr. Hall typed for a moment before changing the subject. "So, we haven't spoken much about your father yet. Are you ready to tell me about him?"

Zoey looked away. "There's not much to say."

"You mentioned that you grew apart over the years. How did that happen?"

"Uh, I can't really explain all that well... just at one point he stopped being," Zoey paused, "himself I guess."

"What do you mean?" Dr. Hall questioned."

Zoey thought back to her father yelling at her when she was a teenager. Shortly after her mom passed, his mood tremendously changed and after a while, she couldn't take it. He became so angry at the world, it made it hard for Zoey to effectively communicate her feelings to him. There were times when she wondered if her father realized how she felt. Even though they both lost Leanne, it sometimes felt like he forgot that it was her mother that died and not just his wife.

"It's hard to explain," Zoey sighed. "He just got really mad at life after my mom died. I get that he's mad but... he just sort of took it out on me a lot. I mean, I know he doesn't mean it but after a while, it seemed like he stopped caring about my feelings or maybe he just forgot about them. I don't know..." her voice trailed off.

Hearing herself speak about her father in such a way estranged her. In fact, she didn't even anticipate the words coming out.

"Have you told him about how you feel when he acts that way?" Dr. Hall asked.

"Oh yeah, several times. It's a pointless conversation. He's stuck in his ways. He's mad at life. I get it."

Dr. Hall nodded. "Have you started taking the anxiety medication I gave you yet?"

"Uh, yes..." Zoey lied.

Dr. Hall gave her a look as if she knew she was lying but didn't question it. Instead, she typed for a good minute in silence while Zoey imagined chucking the laptop out of the window behind her.

"Can you please stop typing?" Zoey asked more so in a demand than a question.

"Were you able to log on to the computer?" Dr. Hall asked as she stopped.

"Yeah, but it didn't help much. I still can't remember what Mr. Davis looks like; that's the name of my client. All I got was his phone number, but I don't think I should contact him."

"Why not?" Dr. Hall questioned.

"Because what am I going to say? That I'm in a mental hospital? That sounds terrible."

"You're in the behavioral section of the hospital... not a mental hospital. That is the proper term," Dr. Hall corrected her, "but no, I don't think you should say that. You could try emailing him instead of calling."

"Yeah, but I still don't know what to say," Zoey groaned.

"I've always learned that honesty works best in most situations. Go with your gut.

Think it over and I'm sure you'll figure out what to do," Dr. Hall smiled.

She's full of suggestions but no real answers.

"Aren't you supposed to tell me what to do instead? Isn't that your job? To tell me how to handle this?" Zoey gave her an odd look.

"I don't tell anyone what to do, I only try to help," Dr. Hall smiled. "Keep writing in your notebook, Zoey. Our session is over today unless you would like to talk about anything else, I'll see you tomorrow."

I rather never see you again and go home.

Zoey didn't believe there was any use to argue so she left the office and went straight to the cafeteria, realizing that Dr. Hall and the staff were there to only listen and give advice which she didn't want. What she did want, was an answer as to why she ran barefoot into a police station calling out for her dead mom, and why she could not remember doing any of it.

8:00 P.M.

On her way out of the cafeteria after eating dinner, the nurse stopped Zoey to give her the medication, and once again Zoey fooled her into thinking that she swallowed it. Instead, she hid it under her tongue and immediately spit it into the toilet when she got back to her room.

She went over to her nightstand and pulled out her planner, then turned to the week of.

Sunday, I remember reading for half an hour in the morning, and then I went to photograph the Gonzalez family. I think I got there a little after 11 in the morning… we shot for about two hours, then I had the rest of the day to edit.

Frustrated that she still couldn't remember anything the following day, Zoey began to hyperventilate. She dropped to her knees on the floor, put her hands in a prayer position and took a deep breath.

The last time she prayed to God was when she was fourteen years old. Her parents were Christians but were not religious their whole lives. It wasn't until during the few years before Leanne died, when she decided to turn to prayer and teach Zoey and her father to do so as well. Zoey kept her relationship with God for about two years until one day shortly after her mother died, she suddenly stopped praying and the relationship with him diminished. She eventually stopped talking to him and began praying to her mom instead.

"Mom please, send me a sign. Something... help me out of this mess... I don't remember anything. I don't know why I told the cops that I saw you..."

Tears now streamed down her face. Her sadness began turning to anger and without even thinking, she clenched her fists and banged them against the carpet.

"Why aren't you here... why aren't you..." Zoey whaled like a two-year-old, "why aren't you-?"

She stopped crying as a sense of Déjà vu swept over her and she stopped hitting the carpet.

Why does this feel so familiar?

She closed her eyes and could suddenly picture herself sitting in her car. She was parked in the cemetery parking lot, crying out to her mother and slamming her hands against the steering wheel, in the same way as she just was, in her hospital room.

I did this before...

In the next moment, she thought of sitting on the grass in front of her mother's name. Rain clouds hovered over her. Tears streamed down her face as she wiped them with the sleeve of her jacket.

"When... when did I go to the cemetery?" she asked herself as she could not understand what she was just thinking of.

It was raining there… and it was raining when I went to the police… it's raining right now…

Something about the rain was nagging Zoey… and something about the cemetery feeling so familiar but not clear in her memory made her uneasy.

She opened her notebook and pulled out all the pieces of paper that she had written on, then laid them across the floor in a detective-like fashion.

I have to figure this out. If I don't, then, who will?

CHAPTER 5

DEC 15th

7:00 A.M.

Zoey woke up to the horrible sound of Kelsey's tone-deaf singing.

"Breakfast time, breakfast time!" she hollered through the halls in an opera like tone.

"Shut up!" a patient yelled out from another room.

"You shut up! BREAKFAST TIME!" Kelsey shouted back.

Why is this happening?

"Breakfast tiiiime!" Kelsey sang as she pushed open Zoey's door.

Zoey threw a pillow at her, but Kelsey crouched down, dodging it just in time.

"Are you serious? Get out of here!"

"What did you say to me, missy? I'm older than you, you know that?!"

Kelsey walked forward, hands on her hips. She was clearly trying to provoke Zoey but instead, all she was doing was portraying herself as a crackhead in need of her crack.

"I said, what did you say, huh?" she repeated louder.

Zoey got up from her bed and stepped close to Kelsey's face.

"I said, get out of my room!"

Kelsey laughed, then picked up one of Zoey's notes that she left on the floor from the night before.

"Ooooh, what's this? Dream number one-"

"Give that back!" Zoey snatched the note out of her hand. "Get out!"

Kelsey laughed again and then kicked at the rest of the notes on the floor.

"Are you kidding me!?"

Zoey was in shock. She threw the note down to the ground and pushed Kelsey, who caught herself by falling against the bed. She leaped towards Zoey and tried to push her down, but Zoey anticipated her attack and ducked out of the way just in time.

"Stupid notes!" Kelsey laughed again as she went to kick at them.

Just as she did, Zoey grabbed her by the hair and pulled her down to the ground.

"HELP SHE'S ATTACKING ME!!!" Kelsey cried out.

"Oh, shut up!" Zoey groaned.

She dropped on top of her, pinning her down by the knee.

"Get off me! Help she's hurting me!" Kelsey kept yelling.

Just as Zoey raised her hand in the air, ready to slap Kelsey's face, Tee came running into the room and yanked her off. He stood Kelsey up and went to pull her out of the room while she struggled to get out of his grip.

"Stay out of my room next time!" Zoey grunted, "AND CLOSE MY DOOR!"

"No more closed-door privileges for you," Tee answered.

"Are you serious? She was the one who just walked in... WHEN MY DOOR WAS ACTUALLY CLOSED!"

Zoey felt her face grow hot.

"You shouldn't have got into a fight. Door stays open," he said and started to walk away.

"Even when I'm sleeping?!" Zoey asked shockingly, but Tee was already gone.

Great. Now I really can't get away from anyone.

Zoey picked up the notes off the floor and put them under her mattress. Her stomach started rumbling but she wasn't sure if it was nauseous from the fight, the lack of sleep she's had in the past few days, or if she was just hungry.

I can't stay in this room. I need to keep myself distracted before I really go crazy.

Evading Tee's orders, she shut the door behind her as she walked out of her room and headed to the cafeteria.

Just as she was about to turn the corner by Derek's room, he popped out of the doorway and whispered, "they're coming to get you... they're coming."

Don't make eye contact... don't make eye contact.

Zoey continued walking around the corner and ran right into Destiny.

"Where are you going?" she asked.

"To go eat..." Zoey sighed.

"Great! I'll join you!" Destiny clapped.

Just what I need.

She hooked her arm around Zoey's and skipped to the cafeteria, causing Zoey to forcefully walk faster.

As soon as they got their food and sat down, the nurse came up to them.

"Would you like to take your medication this morning or later?" she asked Zoey.

"Now's fine," Zoey mumbled as she took the pill from the nurse and examined it.

Maybe this might actually help me.

Zoey's mind felt like it was on fire from confusion. She hated taking medication but right now, she decided against her normal choice hoping it might help her.

Well, if anything goes wrong, I'm in the right place, I guess.

She swallowed the pill for the first time and immediately regretted her decision. The nurse turned to Destiny and dropped a larger pill in her hand.

"Oh! my favorite candy!" Destiny took it, then the nurse walked back to her chair.

"I heard she has 27 cats at home," Destiny giggled.

"I wouldn't doubt it," Zoey paused, "wait-did you actually swallow that pill?"

"Oh yeah, I like this one. I think it gives me energy!" Destiny said cheerfully.

I don't think energy is what you need.

"So, I got into a fight with Kelsey today," Zoey volunteered.

"Oh, do tell!" Destiny said with her mouth full of food. "I love a good brawl! Tell me all the chaotic details! Did it involve her tone-deaf of a voice she calls singing? I've gotten into it with her twice before… after the second time she learned not to mess with all this." Destiny flipped her hair, immensely proud of whatever she did to Kelsey.

"Yeah, well kind of. It was her fault though. She just opened my door without knocking then started messing with my notes. I got mad and pushed her and then Tee had to pull me off her," Zoey shrugged.

"Did he stop your closed-door privileges?"

"Yeah, how'd you know?"

Destiny tilted her head slightly to the left and pouted her lips.

"Girl, I told you. I KNOW what goes on here."

That is not something to be proud of.

"Of course, you do," Zoey smirked.

Just then, Tina and Lisa walked over and sat next to the girls with their trays of food. Lisa hummed as she held a forkful of bacon up to her doll's mouth.

"Why are you always trying to feed her? She's not real," Tina scoffed, who looked more irritable than normal.

"You should be nicer to her," Destiny chimed in.

"Don't tell me how to talk to my sister," Tina snapped back.

"Hey, don't take your anger out on me, my pretty," Destiny held her hands in the air like she was under arrest.

"Ugh!" Tina groaned. "I just can't take it here anymore. We're adults and they treat us like children."

Destiny looked across the table at Lisa, "and how old is Lisa again?"

"She's a different story!" Tina said in a more defensive and louder tone.

"Well, I'm going to go back to my room," Zoey said as she went to stand up, but a wave of dizziness crept upon her.

Destiny noticed her stumble and she stood up immediately to help her.

"Oh, I'll help you Zo Zo," she volunteered.

Too weak to argue, Zoey allowed Destiny to help and escort her back to her room.

As soon as her head hit the pillow, she fell right to sleep.

11:00 A.M.

"Zo Zo! Wake up, wake up!" Destiny was kneeling at Zoey's bed, nudging her arm. "Your sister is on the phone!"

Zoey woke up, still feeling woozy. She wondered what was in that medicine she took. Whatever it was, she didn't plan on taking it again. It was hard for her to stand as she tried to get out of bed, so Destiny helped lead her down the hallway.

When they got there, Derek had the phone to his ear.

"You have to listen to us. We're warning you!" he whispered.

"Excuse me, that phone calls for me," Zoey said, trying not to trigger any personalities she didn't want to see.

Instead of answering her, he turned his back against her and continued repeating into the phone. Destiny stepped right into his face and turned him around by his shoulder. "Hey, give Zo Zo the phone right now!" she demanded.

Derek instantly screamed and dropped the phone, then ran quickly back to his room.

"That's how you handle that!" Destiny said, wiping her hands together as if there were dust on them. She picked up the phone and handed it to Zoey.

"See you later, Zo Zo!"

Zoey put the phone to her ear. "Hi," she sighed.

"I need to get you out of there right now! Who was that?!" Alex gasped.

"I'm fine. It was Derek. He's crazy... along with everyone else I guess," Zoey dragged her words realizing that what she was saying didn't sound comforting.

"Zoey, I'm worried about you. Your dad called. He said he was calling you, but you haven't answered for a few days, so I figured you didn't tell him?"

"No, not yet."

"You need to. He's worried. He's going to keep calling me, you know that."

"I know," Zoey sighed. "I just don't know what to say. You know, I keep thinking, why would I go into the police station? I literally look like I was on drugs or something in that video. You saw it! I don't even recognize myself... and I still don't get why I have my purse but not my shoes... I'm so confused."

"What are the Doctors saying?" Alex asked.

"I'm only talking to one. Her name's Dr. Hall. She gave me anxiety medicine, which completely messed me up this morning. I got so dizzy and it knocked me out for about two hours. I only woke up because you called. I'm still drowsy... I'm pretty sure that this doctor just thinks that I belong here because my mom died. She makes me talk about my family and stuff. It's annoying. I just want to get out of here."

"Hmm." Alex sounded like she had a thought but didn't want to say it.

"Say it..." Zoey insisted.

"Well, Christmas is coming up... you know how you can get around these times. It's understandable."

"Yeah, yeah... I know I get all depressed around the holidays but... I don't know why that would have anything to do with me forgetting a whole day. I'm not like the other patients. I shouldn't be here... I'm really trying not to freak out."

"I know you don't belong there. I'm going to come by tonight," Alex said. "I just thought I'd call to see how you were doing and tell you about your dad. We'll figure this out."

"Thanks," Zoey sighed. "I'm going back to my room to fix my notes. Oh yeah, I got into a fight with another woman here, but she started it."

"You mean an actual fistfight?" Alex was shocked.

"Yeah, I'll tell you more about that when I see you."

"Okay, do you want me to stop by your apartment and get you anything?" Alex asked.

Zoey looked down at her tied-up hospital gown and sweats.

"Actually, yeah. Can you bring me a pair of leggings or sweatpants and a shirt or sweater or something? I've been wearing this uncomfortable hospital gown as a shirt and it's annoying."

"Of course, sis. I'll see you later," Alex said.

When Zoey got back to her room, she immediately pulled out all her ripped-up notes from under the mattress, which she was thankful that Kelsey didn't succeed in damaging them enough to be unreadable. She looked at the note with her client's phone number and wondered, "what's the worst thing that could happen?"

So, Zoey took the paper and walked back to the hallway phone. She took a deep breath and then dialed his phone number. It rang only twice before a sudden rush of anxiety hit her and she quickly hung up the phone.

Nope... Bad idea, nope, I shouldn't do this... I don't even know what I'm gonna say to him.

Just as Zoey turned around to head back to her room the phone rang, and her heart felt like it dropped to her feet. She inhaled deeply, then exhaled before turning around to answer. She slowly brought the phone to her ear. "Hel-- Hello?" she stammered.

"Hi, yes someone just called from this number. This is Dr. Davis."

So, Mr. Davis is Dr. Davis... I don't remember having a doctor as a client.

"Hello?" Dr. Davis asked again.

"Uh, yeah sorry. Hi, Dr. Davis," Zoey said as she closed her eyes. "Um, this is Zoey. I was your photographer for the Christmas shoot the other day..."

"Oh yes, Hi Zoey! I can't wait to see the final pictures. I am glad you chose to shoot inside rather than outside. You were right, that Florida rain just sneaks up on you," he chuckled. "I'm still getting used to it. You would think that I would be after a year of living here already. Anyway, I haven't had a chance to email you and thank you for such a nice shoot. I know my wife wasn't feeling the greatest, but she was still incredibly happy with the shots you showed us before you left."

I have no idea what you're talking about...

"Oh yeah, they did come out great and that's really no problem at all," Zoey gulped. "Everyone was great. It was a pleasure to photograph your family... Well, I was just calling to touch base and let you know that I'm still in the editing process and I will let you know when I am done."

"Oh great, thank you again. Are you okay though? My caller ID read as the number from the hospital. I thought a colleague was calling me," he said.

"Oh yeah, I'm fine. I, uh-- I'm at the hospital but not for me. I'm visiting a friend, it's nothing serious. My phone died so I'm trying to multi-task and get some work done. I was looking over your photos on my laptop and realized I hadn't touched base with you yet so I used the hospital phone… the photos should be ready soon."

"Oh, I see. Okay, well I hope your friend feels better. Thanks again for calling," Dr. Davis said.

"No problem, I'll be in touch in a few days," Zoey hung up, hoping that what she just said would come true. She put her note and pen up against the wall and wrote:

Mr. Davis is Dr. Davis. I finished the photoshoot, it was indoors, Dr. Davis's wife was sick.

"My turn!" Kelsey tapped on Zoey's shoulder.

"Move out of my way!"

This girl, again.

Zoey slapped Kelsey's hand off her shoulder like it was a fly. "Don't touch me," she warned, then put her note and pen back in her sweatpants pocket.

She went to walk away from the phone, but Kelsey poked her other shoulder as she did so.

"What is wrong with you?" Zoey turned around furious; fists clenched.

Kelsey laughed maniacally, and pushed Zoey, who was unexpecting it and fell on her back. "HAHAHAHA," she continued to laugh louder as she stood over her.

I'm going to kill this girl!

Zoey jolted up from rage and grabbed Kelsey by her neck. She yanked her down in one swift motion and kicked her right in the stomach. Tee came running from around the corner and grabbed Zoey from her armpits, tearing her away from Kelsey while another guard grabbed Kelsey. Zoey stopped trying to squirm out of Tee's grip and began to calm down.

"Okay, I'm fine. Let me go. I stopped," she said breathlessly.

Tee lightened his grip but still held on to one arm as he started to lead her down the hallway.

"Back to your room, let's go," he said.

"What about lunch? You can't deprive me of food," Zoey said hastily as he pulled her down the hallway.

"You can eat it in your room. Door still stays open," he said right as they approached her room.

I'm going to lose my mind here… these people are going to make me actually go crazy!

Tee left Zoey in her room and she immediately began pacing back and forth, thinking about what Dr. Davis said to her on the phone. Lightning suddenly struck outside and the lights in the hospital flickered. Screams and cries were immediately heard from the other patients as soon as it happened.

"It's okay, it's okay everyone. Just a bad storm. Everything's fine," Debra called out through the halls.

Just a minute later, the lights came back but some patients were still crying.

I can't believe this is happening to me.

Zoey laid in bed and pulled the blanket over her head. The sound of the thunder and rain started to make her think about the photo-shoot.

"I feel like I would remember someone getting sick..." she thought out loud. It was rare that Zoey encountered a sick client during her shoots. They would most of the time reschedule or if anything, it was normally the children who were sick. It was also uncommon to have a doctor as a client as well.

"Here's your lunch," Tee's voice shifted Zoey away from her thoughts when he walked in her room, holding a plate with a hot dog and fries on it.

Zoey rolled her eyes and muttered, "thanks."

He put the plate beside her on the bed and went to walk out of the room, but she stopped him before he got to the door. "Wait, so what does this mean? I'm stuck here for the rest of the time?" she asked.

"Only for today," he said.

"Why? Because I defended myself?"

"No, because you got into a fight," he answered.

"Kelsey's the one that should be locked up and you know it!" Zoey insisted.

"You are both on punishment. I'll come to get you for your session later and bring your dinner to you after. If you listen, then you will be free tomorrow. Think you can handle that?" he said as he crossed his arms.

"Sure," Zoey muttered.

"Remember, the door stays open for the night too," he grinned.

Again, Zoey couldn't tell if he was being genuine or sarcastic.

Instead of eating, she decided to take a shower, then got dressed in the same sweats and hospital gown that she was wearing before. The smell from the hot dog started to make her feel sick, so she took the plate and put it in the sink of the bathroom and closed the door. She got in bed and pulled the covers over her eyes, hoping that she would somehow fall asleep until Alex showed up.

8:00 P.M.

Zoey's wish came true. She ended up falling asleep shortly after her shower and ended up missing her session and dinner. She woke up just as Alex walked in and dropped a large tote bag filled with a week's worth of sweatpants, leggings, a few sweatshirts, and T-shirts on Zoey's bed.

"I didn't think you'd bring me half my wardrobe," Zoey joked as she looked through the bag.

"I don't know. I wanted to be thorough," Alex shrugged. She looked around Zoey's room. "At least you have a clock and a bathroom in here."

"Well, hopefully I'll be out of this place tomorrow..." Zoey sighed, "I'm sick of this room."

"I have something that might cheer you up," Alex said as she pulled a folded piece of paper out of her jean pocket. She handed it to Zoey.

"When I went back to your apartment, I noticed that your laptop was in sleep mode, so I went on it."

Zoey gave her a worried look.

"Don't worry, I didn't mess anything up," Alex reassured her. She was terrible with computers, and she knew it.

"I know that I suck at technology, but I thought I'd turn your laptop on just to see if anything was on there that could help and when I did, the files to your hard drive were up. I went into your client folder and found the pictures you took on Monday! I printed one of them out."

Zoey was confused as to how Alex maneuvered through her files without messing anything up but also greatly relieved that she was about to look at something from Monday.

She frantically unfolded the paper and looked into the eyes of a mother, father, and a teenage daughter. The family posed in front of a large white Christmas tree draped in beautiful silver tinsel, classy ornaments, and green garland. Dr. Davis stood tall in a dark green business suit. His wife wore a beautiful formal long-sleeved burgundy dress doused in sequins.

Those sequins are going to be annoying to edit.

The daughter was just a bit taller than her mother and she also wore a long-sleeved dress, but without sequins and more of a cherry red color.

"Anything?" Alex asked.

"I'm thinking… I don't know. I called him earlier. I'm trying to put a face to his voice… I didn't get a chance to tell you because I called him after I called you and then I got into another fight with Kelsey."

"Wait, What?" Alex asked, confused.

"I called him after I got off the phone with you. Actually, he called me… well after I called him."

"Wh-- what?" Alex repeated.

She was now looking at Zoey like she really belonged in the hospital.

For the remainder of the visiting hour, Zoey told her about the fights with Kelsey and how well she lied to Dr. Davis, then they went over her notes together. When Alex read the note about Zoey sitting in the cemetery, she asked which jacket it was that she pictured herself wearing.

After a moment, "It had to be my work jacket. It doubles as a raincoat… I guess that would make sense," Zoey said. "But I don't actually remember sitting there. It was like a vision or I don't know how to describe it."

Zoey never thought that she could feel so many emotions at the same time. She and Alex both continued to try and brainstorm what could have happened and before they knew it, the hour suddenly was over. It was time for Alex to leave and Zoey walked her to the entrance, then went back to her room.

She immediately went through the bag of clothes that Alex brought her and changed into a blue T-shirt and a pair of black leggings. Instead of going to bed, she paced back and forth with a fixated glance on the Davis's as she held the photo in her hand.

The three of them were standing close together. Dr. Davis had a commercial smile as he stood proudly with one arm around his wife's waist and his other hand on his daughter's shoulder. The daughter posed with her hands on her hips and her brunette hair was placed into a high ballerina-like bun. Her mother's hair color was just a bit darker and was styled down in beautiful waves that reached her shoulders. She smiled with just her bright red lips pressed together.

Zoey looked at the closed curtains on the balcony behind them and wished they were open. It always makes for a better view. She looked at the white Christmas tree surrounded by red and green wrapped presents underneath it and exchanged her look back to Mrs. Davis again.

This time, she spotted what looked like a part of a scar on her chest. Because of the style of the dress, it was hard to see the entire thing but for some reason, it reminded Zoey of her own mother's scar.

She had one sort of similar on her neck. The scar was from what doctors called a *port* that had been inserted for chemotherapy treatments. The thought of it made Zoey think back to the pain in her mother's face every time a nurse stuck it with a needle. It was way too often that Zoey could recall being at her mother's bedside, trying to calm her down during the times when she would receive her treatments. Her father thankfully, was always beside them as Zoey could never recall seeing him break down or anything of that matter.

During the whole time that her mother was sick, Zoey can only remember him being strong, for everyone.

Thinking about her dad made Zoey look at Dr. Davis. His smile was bright, yet not forced but it didn't seem truly happy. She wondered what kind of doctor he was and what emotions were being kept back behind that smile.

"If only you three could tell me what happened," Zoey sighed as she kept her eyes locked on the family photo.

CHAPTER 6

DEC 16th

7:30 A.M.

"Hello, so nice to meet you! I'm sorry, my daughter is still getting ready and my wife's not feeling too good at the moment. Would you mind giving us a few more minutes?"

"Of course, no problem at all. I have to set up anyway. Take as much time as you need."

Zoey placed her equipment down, then walked over to the balcony near the tree and peeked out of the curtain. The lightning lit up the dark blue sky and the rain started to roll in.

"BLEH, BLEH!"

Mrs. Davis must be really, sick...

The sounds of puking from the bathroom became louder, followed by more thunder.

Suddenly the lights flickered, and Zoey felt her body shake.

"Zo Zo!! Wake up!"

Who is —

"NURSEEEE!!!!"

The sound of Destiny's voice jolted Zoey awake. "Huh?" She muttered as she sat up.

It took a minute to realize that she was still in the hospital as she tried to catch her breath.

"Zo Zo! Oh, my lanta, are you okay?!" Destiny gasped. "I was coming to see if you were awake and then when I got here, you were whining in your sleep! I thought something was wrong!"

Zoey fumbled around her bed, "where is it!?"

"Where's what?" Destiny tilted her head.

"My notebook," Zoey said as she found it under her pillow. "Now where's the pen?"

"Here," Destiny held out the pen with a skeptical look on her face. "What happened? Did you remember something? Were you dreaming?! Is that why you were freaking out?!"

"The photoshoot... I remember it raining now... and the layout of the living room," Zoey said out loud as she wrote it down in her notes.

Destiny sat at the edge of the bed, dangling her legs back and forth as she watched Zoey write.

"And what else happened in this thrillerish dream of yours?" she curiously asked.

"I was at my client's house for their photoshoot... the wife was sick," Zoey was more so thinking out loud than explaining it to Destiny.

"I'm trying to remember being there. I remember the balcony and the rain... but I don't remember her getting sick ... I remember everything else I just dreamt... but not Mrs. Davis being sick."

"Would you REALLY remember that though?" Destiny asked as she jumped off the bed carefree, "Come on! Let's go eat! I'm starving."

"I'm in lockdown. I can't," Zoey groaned.

117

"Not anymore, you're not. It was only for a day, silly. It's already 7:30 in the morning!"

Destiny pulled Zoey's arm to get her off the bed, "let's go!"

Zoey looked down at her notes and decided not to obsess over what she just dreamt. Her head was beginning to pound which made it hard to focus.

I can't do anything else here… and I can't focus on anything with this damn headache.

"Fine," she sighed and followed Destiny out of the room.

The girls walked into the cafeteria and got their breakfast. Zoey started to walk over to Lisa and Tina's table, but Destiny didn't follow.

"I'll catch up with you in a little bit, my pretty," she said, then skipped over to the next table where Will was sitting.

She's never going to give up…

"Hi Will, can I do you the pleasure of blessing you with my presence?" Destiny asked, standing in front of him with her plate of eggs.

"I don't care," Will shrugged as he swallowed a whole piece of bacon.

Instead of sitting in front of him, she walked around the table and plopped herself right beside him. "How's it gooooo-inng?"

"Fine," he mumbled with a mouthful of food.

She moved the eggs around her plate with a fork. "How ya liking it in here?"

Will gave her a peculiar look. "Is that a serious question?"

"Your hair's so curly!" She slid closer. "Can I touch it?"

Will shrugged just as Destiny was already starting to pull one of his curls down. She watched it straighten and then bounce back up to his neckline.

"Such vivacious curly, gorgeous hair," she giggled. "I wish my hair were as curly as yours! Your hair is like, spirally curly unlike my big curls!"

Will rolled his eyes and continued to keep eating, without answering her. Destiny sighed extra loudly and pushed her tray forward. She rested her elbows on the table.

"Sooo, what happened to you? Huh? I still don't know your story. Who made you come here? Tell me about all your demons, Will."

He dropped his fork and glared at her. "Why are you talking to me?"

"You seemed lonely," she shrugged.

"And that's how I want to stay," he muttered and stood up from the table.

He took his tray to the garbage can, dumped the remnants of his food, and walked out of the cafeteria.

"Ugh!" Destiny grunted and slammed her tray off the table.

Zoey, Tina, and Lisa immediately jumped up from their seats and rushed over to her.

"He didn't want to-- to talk to me," Destiny stammered. "What is wrong with me ladies? I'm a beauty. Why doesn't he see that?"

"He just doesn't seem like the type to want to talk to anyone... it's not you," Zoey tried comforting her.

"Please don't cry," Lisa pleaded, as she was on the verge of tears herself. "I don't like to see people cry."

Destiny wiped her tears away, stood up, and did her signature hair flip.

"I'm going to go lay down. I don't feel good." She tugged at her clothes, straightened up, and strutted out of the room like she was on a runway.

Zoey watched her model walk away and then looked at Lisa, who was now in full tears while Tina sat beside her, patting her back.

I need to get myself out of here...

Zoey put her tray away and left the cafeteria to go back to her room.

On her way, she decided to stop at the hallway phone and call her dad.

It's now or never.

After just one ring, he answered.

"Hi dad, it's me," she sighed.

"Why are you calling from the hospital? Are you okay?"

Great... He's already worried.

"Kind of... um, well I'm in the behavioral... part of the hospital."

"What the hell are you talking about?" he asked.

Zoey swallowed as she tried to hold back her aggravation. "A psych ward dad."

"But why are you there?" he asked, sounding just as confused as she was.

I'm glad he's not on social media.

"Well, I'm not so sure actually. I'm just as confused as you. The police brought me here because I was looking... I was looking for...

mom… I don't know, it's not a big deal. I'll figure it out. I just didn't want to worry you, so I thought I'd call," Zoey sighed.

"Bu--but wait hold on. This is a big deal, what do you mean?" he asked.

"I thought I saw mom and I was acting… a little crazy at the police station."

"I just, I don't understand Zoey. When did this happen? When can you leave? Why would you think that?"

"A few days ago. They said I can leave when they think I'm ready."

"Okay so-"

Before he could say anything else, Zoey stopped the conversation. "Listen, I'm fine. Don't worry. I'll be out of here soon. I'll call you later. I got to go."

"Are you sure? They can't just keep you there. Can I come to see you?" he asked frantically.

I knew I shouldn't have told him this…

"No, no, I'm fine really. I should be out of here soon."

Her dad sighed, "okay… call me if you need anything."

"Yeah, I will dad. Don't worry. I'll be okay, love you."

Zoey hung up the phone and went back to her room.

2:00 P.M.

Zoey walked into the activity room and felt relieved to see that Kelsey wasn't around.

Lisa and Tina were sitting on the couch, so she went to sit with them. "Hey-"

"-Shh! This is the best part!" Lisa whispered.

"She's seen this movie like a hundred times," Tina rolled her eyes.

There was an animated movie on the screen, which for some reason aggravated Zoey.

Now I'm watching kid movies... I can't sit here...

Zoey got up and walked over to the window.

She looked over to Debra, who was sitting next to Will at the computer desk.

"When can we go outside? It's not raining right now," Zoey asked.

"Maybe tomorrow, honey. Everything is wet out there from earlier. It's not safe," Debra said in her friendly tone.

"Fine. Can I use the computer next?" Zoey asked.

Debra nodded, "you can use it now. Will was just logging off."

Will mumbled something too low for Zoey to understand and reluctantly got up.

Zoey walked over and sat down. She logged into her account, which showed a total of 12 unread emails. Most of them were from clients she photographed the week before, mainly asking for an update on their photos which she didn't know how to reply, so she decided to leave her email and log into her social media. The first thing that she noticed, were the 52 unread notifications that popped up on the right of her screen.

Although she knew that it was a bad idea, Zoey clicked on them and began to scroll through. They all varied from worried friends to random people asking what kind of drugs she took and where they could find them.

I can't believe this is really happening to me...

Just as she was about to click away, she noticed that an old friend from high school shared the video. The status above the post read: **So sad to see this happen to an old friend. I'm praying for you, Zoey!** followed by five sad face emojis.

She clicked play on the 18-second video and cringed as she watched herself yell in front of the police station.

I was barefoot in the rain... my clothes are soaked... why the hell did I do that? Why can't I remember any of this yet?

Zoey replayed the video three times, torturing herself every time she watched.

It was raining just before this video was taken and it was raining at the photoshoot... It was raining at the cemetery...

She hit pause on the video, sat back, and stared at the screen.

Suddenly, lightning struck outside the hospital causing the power to go out for a slight moment which made the computer turn off completely.

"No! Not yet. Are you kidding me?" Zoey grunted in aggravation.

"Sorry honey. Storms coming back. You can go on the computer tomorrow," Debra said.

"I don't want there to be a tomorrow," Zoey shook her head.

"Oh, honey don't say that. There's always tomorrow," Debra smiled innocently.

I need to get up before I punch her.

Zoey got up from her chair, looked around the room and realized that Destiny hadn't come in yet, which was unusual as she was normally everywhere. So, for some reason, Zoey decided to go check on her.

Not sure why I'm doing this… but I'm doing it.

Zoey left the activity room and headed down the hallway. As she went towards Destiny's room, she passed by Miriam who was walking back and forth in front of her room.

"Miriam, why aren't you in the activity room?" Zoey asked.

"Cause they're all schmucks in there! When I get out of this place, they're going to miss me here! Wait until I see my sister again, you wait!" Miriam laughed deviously.

Zoey smirked. "I believe in you," she said and continued her way down the hall.

She reached Destiny's door, which was closed so she knocked softly. After a few seconds, she knocked again but Destiny didn't answer so she opened the door and poked her head in.

"Are you okay?" she asked as she saw Destiny sitting in the corner on the floor with her knees up to her chest. "I just wanted to check on you. Don't let Will upset you, Destiny."

Destiny lifted her head and sniffled. "Guys never like me. I will forever be a damsel."

This girl has bad self-esteem issues...

"You can't sit in here all day," Zoey said to cheer her up.

Destiny wiped her teary eyes and leaped to her feet in an instant mood change. She flipped her hair. "You're right Zo Zo! I'm not going to let a man get me down! Come on let's go!"

She locked her arm in Zoey's and led her back to the activity room.

5:00 P.M.

"So, there was a comment you made to Debra that I'd like to talk about with you," Dr. Hall said as she sat across from Zoey.

Zoey shook her head, confused. "What comment?"

Dr. Hall gave her a sincere look and widened her eyes a bit.

"You said the words: Hopefully, there won't be a tomorrow."

Are you kidding me?!

"Oh wow... uh no, oh my god! That's not what I meant. I said it as in; hopefully, I'm not HERE tomorrow," Zoey said, emphasizing the word: here.

Dr. Hall raised an eyebrow.

"No, no, no, not like that! Oh my god!" Zoey exclaimed. "I mean here in this hospital. I meant hopefully, I'm not still here in this hospital tomorrow and that I'm HOME instead."

Deep breaths... Deep breaths...

Dr. Hall sat back in her chair. "What would you be doing at home right now?"

Is she serious?

"Uh, my job... I have people waiting on me," Zoey tried to answer in a way where she didn't sound both confused and annoyed.

"But what about besides work?" Dr. Hall asked.

"I don't know. Clean my apartment... work out... there's a ton of things I can be doing."

"Exercise is great for you but what about your hobbies?" Dr. Hall asked.

"I don't know. I don't really have any hobbies..." Zoey gave her an odd look. "Why?"

"You've spoken a lot about your work but not much about your personal life. I can tell that you're very focused driven, but I'd like to know more about you. Work can't be your whole life."

"Mm, no I think it is, actually. I've never thought about it until you started questioning me," Zoey scoffed.

"Maybe that's a good thing," Dr. Hall smiled. "Do you ever take photos just for fun?"

"I used to. I haven't done that in a while though..." Zoey's voice trailed off as she thought about when she first got into photography.

She could remember going out to different areas in her free time and taking pictures of anything she thought was photo worthy.

"It sounds like you need to make more time for yourself," Dr. Hall concluded.

"Well, I'm getting all the time in the world now, thanks to you and the police," Zoey smirked.

Dr. Hall smiled, ignoring her sarcasm. "You're absolutely right. You do have all the time you want here. Now you can focus on yourself with no work distractions."

I'm going to slap that stupid smile off your face.

"But what about my clients?!" Zoey exclaimed, legs shaking in her seat.

"You need to worry less about your clients and more about you. I would suggest that you contact them and just be honest. I want you to focus on relaxing more. How's the medicine working for you?"

"It's going fine," Zoey sighed, "but I get tired from it."

"Sleep is good. It's when your brain rests," Dr. Hall said.

She's really pushing this relaxing concept.

"Okay, I get it," Zoey rolled her eyes. "I'll try to relax more but you have to understand, not remembering what I did the day that I got here is driving me crazy. It's scaring me. I don't understand how I lost my memory for a whole day... what if I never remember anything at all?"

Dr. Hall pressed her lips together in a half-smile. "I can't understand how you're feeling but I can listen and offer my advice. I'm sure whatever you did that day is going to come back to you. Just try not to force it. Let it come naturally."

"Easy for you to say," Zoey mumbled.

Dr. Hall typed something on her laptop, then turned her attention back to Zoey.

"My suggestion for you is to make nice with others, including Kelsey and work on your mental health while you're here. Who knows? You might learn something new."

Zoey sat up in her chair. "Okay, I've been here five days already. What else do I need to do to get out of here? I'm not a danger to myself or anyone. Why can't I go home yet?"

Dr. Hall leaned forward on her desk and clasped her hands together, "The fact that you don't remember a day that led you to believe your mom is alive and landed you here in this hospital, is the very reason why you need to stay, Zoey."

"Ugh!" Zoey slumped back down in her chair. She looked up at the ceiling.

"Get me out of here! Please!" she cried out.

Dr. Hall nodded in approval. "Talking to god works too! Are you religious?"

Zoey rubbed her forehead. "No, I'm not talking to god. I'm talking to my mom. I don't talk to god anymore."

"Oh, why is that?" Dr. Hall questioned.

"Why do you think?" Zoey snapped.

Dr. Hall didn't say anything but shrug her shoulders.

Zoey stood up. "I don't talk to him anymore because he took my mom away. Anyway, I'm getting hungry. I think I'm going to go to the cafeteria early and wait for dinner," she said through a forced smile.

Dr. Hall smiled back, "Okay Zoey, enjoy your dinner. I'll see you tomorrow."

I can't wait until I never hear those words again.

6:00 P.M.

Zoey opened her palm as the cafeteria nurse approached her table. She smiled, hoping that it didn't look forced, and put the pill into her mouth.

She looks like a Becky to me. I wonder what her name is.

The nurse walked away while Zoey discreetly took the pill out of her mouth, then put it under her food tray.

Just as she continued to eat, Lisa, Tina, and Destiny walked into the cafeteria. Within minutes, more patients followed, and Zoey watched them all pile in one after another.

Kelsey's definitely schizo. Miriam's just an old lady who probably didn't deserve what she went through. Derek, well it's very apparent why he's here... I don't belong with any of these people... why am I still in this place?

Zoey's thoughts transitioned back to the cell phone video and out of sudden anger, she spontaneously threw her fork across the room.

"Nice shot," Destiny said as she walked up to her table with Lisa and Tina.

Just as they began to sit down, they all heard the sound of a tray falling to the ground and turned around to see Kelsey in the lunch line, standing over her food on the floor.

Not even a minute later, two guards came running into the cafeteria towards her and grabbed her by the arms, then dragged her away as she struggled to get out of their grip.

I CAN'T BELIEVE THIS IS MY REALITY RIGHT NOW...

CHAPTER 7

DEC 17th

4:00 AM

"I saw her, I swear! You need to help me find her, please!" Zoey shouted as she banged her fists on the hardwood table.

"Ma'am, please calm down," the woman in front of her asked politely.

"NOOO!" Zoey shot up from the table. "YOU HAVE TO FIND HER! PLEASE! She was just around the corner... then I lost her. I haven't seen her in so long... she's alive now! My mom's alive!"

Suddenly she felt something cold against her wrists.

"Relax, relax, relax."

"NO!!!"

"Relax... Relax," the woman repeated as she walked towards her slowly. "Stay still."

A second later, an instant pain shot right through Zoey's shoulder; the same pain she felt the first time she woke up in the hospital.

Oh no, not again... please no...

Zoey's eyes drifted awake just in time to see a nurse pulling a needle out of her arm and Tee lifting his grip off her wrists.

A few seconds later, she fell right back to sleep.

10:00 A.M.

Zoey woke up with probably the biggest headache she ever had in her life. Her shoulder felt like it got punched several times and her wrists were sore. She looked down at her hands and thought back to her dream.

"I was yelling at her... oh my god!" she gasped as the soreness on her wrists from Tee's grip suddenly reminded her of the pain from the handcuffs at the police station.

She found her notebook under her pillow, turned to a new page, and began writing as she thought out loud.

"The cop wouldn't listen to me and I got mad... I got mad that they wouldn't look for my mom... but she-- she's dead... why was I looking for her?"

Zoey examined her shoulder.

"I don't belong here. I shouldn't act this way... And I shouldn't be getting knocked out with horse tranquilizer needles, either!"

She stomped over to the bathroom, splashed her face with cold water, and stared at her reflection.

Just get through lunch, activity time and then session and this will all be over soon...

2:00 P.M.

"Zoey! You're just in time for my acapella!" Lisa called out as soon as she saw her walk into the activity room. She jumped onto the couch and cleared her throat.

"Mm-mm-mm. I'm ready Debra!"

"Okay here we go," Debra said, excitedly. She hit play on a Whitney Houston performance video on the computer and turned up the volume.

"If I should stay... I would only be in your way, so I'll go," Lisa sang in her childish voice that didn't match with Whitney's at all. She jumped off the couch and grabbed Tina's hands, who promptly joined in, "You, my darling you-"

"-so goodbye, please don't cry," Destiny chimed in, spreading her arms out dramatically as she danced her way towards the sisters.

Zoey turned around to go back to her room but bumped right into Dr. Hall.

"Afternoon, Zoey," she said. "Why don't you join them?"

"Um, not really my style..." Zoey answered as she stared at the girls.

Dr. Hall smiled, then went over to the table, grabbed a chair, and dragged it to the middle of the floor, telling Debra to turn off the video.

"More Whitney!!" shouted a patient as soon as the music turned off.

"No more Whitney. It's time for group circle," Dr. Hall said. "Come on everyone, let's sit together. Grab a chair or sit on the floor, whichever you'd like."

Zoey grabbed a chair and placed it as far away from Kelsey as she could. Destiny, Tina, and Lisa all joined by putting their chairs beside her.

"We got your back girl. She knows better than to mess with all of this," Destiny whispered.

This girl is something else...

"So, let's start today's discussion with how we're all feeling at this very moment. Who'd like to start?" Dr. Hall asked the group.

"Me!" Lisa raised her hand. "I'm feeling happy today. Whitney always makes me happy."

"Great! Music in general makes me happy," Dr. Hall agreed. She looked at Tina. "How are you feeling?"

"I'm okay today," Tina mumbled.

"I'm good," Zoey quickly said before Dr. Hall could ask her anything.

"I'm just fan - freaking - tastic! Never better actually," Destiny scoffed.

She crossed her arms and squinted her eyes towards Will, who was sitting next to Dr. Hall.

She's not going to give up.

"Would anyone else like to share?" Dr. Hall asked.

After a moment passed by without anyone answering, Dr. Hall went on to her next subject.

"We talked last time about what we do when we get those feelings of anxiousness, anger and all those heavy feelings. Now, let's talk about why we feel them. Would anyone like to share?"

Tina raised her hand. "I don't know why I get angry. It makes me angry that I get angry for no reason..." she paused, "I start feeling agitated in my body, physically and I just can't stop it and that aggravates me more!"

As Tina spoke about feeling so much aggravation inside of her for no reason, Zoey could not help but think of how much she was starting to relate to her... at least as of lately. Never in her life had she ever gone through so many feelings of despair, defeat, and bewilderment. In fact, Zoey didn't even recall feeling this way when her mother died. She was beginning to feel like something might seriously be wrong with her and it scared her.

Maybe I do belong here...

"I know why I'm angry, I tell ya," Miriam blurted out from the couch, "because of my selfish sister Carole, that's who!"

"Miriam, if you're going to be involved you have to sit in the circle," Dr. Hall said.

"I don't know why you try. She's never going to sit here. She doesn't like any of us," Destiny said as she grinned at Miriam, "which the feeling's mutual by the way."

"See, she's got it right," Miriam said hastily.

"Okay, would anybody else like to share why they get angry or sad?"

"I get sad when Mufasa gets sad," Derek whispered.

"I get angry when other people hurt me!" Kelsey leered as she locked eyes on Zoey.

"Then maybe you should shut your tone-deaf schizo self-up once in a while," Destiny snapped.

Dr. Hall stood up with her palms out as if it would settle the situation. "Okay, I think that's enough for today everyone," she said in her usual calm tone. "I'll see you all later."

Zoey put her chair back and went over to the phone to dial Alex's number. As soon as she answered, Zoey immediately started rambling.

"They're singing in here! Singing! Really singing! It's like I stepped into a musical! And we're talking about our feelings in a group circle... I need to get out of here now! Like right now! I'm losing it for real!"

"Okay, okay, calm down-"

"I can't calm down! Everyone's telling me to calm down but how can I be calm when I'm literally out of control of everything right now?" Zoey gasped.

"You're right... just breathe," Alex said.

Zoey took a deep breath. "Sorry, I don't mean to take it out on you. I'm just really aggravated. I can't believe I'm still here... I can't believe what I just saw."

She shook her head as she pictured the girl's singing off-key around the room.

"Did the photo help you at all? Has anything new come to mind since I've seen you?" Alex asked.

"Sort of... So, I've been having these dreams, only I'm not sure if they're dreams or if I am remembering something that really happened while I'm sleeping," Zoey paused, "I don't remember the Davis's faces or Mrs. Davis getting sick but I dreamt of hearing her throw up... and of their house, which I now remember the layout of... and then I also dreamt of yelling at a cop this morning. When I woke up, I could remember the feeling of the handcuffs against me..." she sighed, "none of this makes sense to me."

"Zoey, that's good!" Alex exclaimed, "you just told me you remember getting handcuffed now... that means it's coming back to you. You didn't remember anything about being at the station before."

"Yeah… slightly, but I still don't know why I told the cops to look for my mom and I still don't remember getting there. Dr. Hall told me that the police said I was acting dangerously. But I don't see why I would even act that way in the first place."

"It's just going to take some time for you to remember everything, I guess," Alex said, "but like I said, at least you remember getting handcuffed."

"I just wish I'd remember everything already so I can figure out how to get out of here. I don't understand why Dr. Hall thinks I'm a danger to myself… I know the video of me doesn't help my case but still, I'm not like the patients in here," Zoey sighed.

"I know you're not. You don't belong there. I just wish I knew what happened to you. I'm surprised I didn't even see the video until you told me about it."

"I," Zoey went to speak but got distracted when she felt someone touch her shoulder. She turned around to see Kelsey standing behind her.

"Time's up. We share around here," Kelsey said while tapping on her imaginary wristwatch.

"What is your problem with me?" Zoey asked.

"Jerry doesn't like you!" Kelsey laughed.

"Who's Jerry?"

"My friend, duh. He's right here," Kelsey gestured beside her.

Oh yeah, she has ghost friends...

"Alex, I'm going to have to call you later," Zoey said into the phone, ignoring Kelsey.

"Please be careful," Alex said.

"I'll do my best," Zoey said into the phone and then hung up.

"All yours, Kelsey," she smirked and walked over to the computer.

She sat down and logged into her email. She clicked on the first unread message, which was from Mrs. Gonzalez who was politely asking for an update on when the pictures will be delivered. More emails followed, from other families who were asking the same thing. Thankfully, none of them seemed to be upset... yet.

I'd like to know when all of your photos will be done too, everyone.

Zoey had no idea what to reply so she decided to log off and not respond to anyone.

I'll just deal with this later... it's not like it matters anymore.

She left the activity room, feeling more hopeless than ever.

5:00 P.M.

"I see that you're making friends," Dr. Hall said to Zoey as they sat across from each other in her office.

"Where did you see that?" Zoey asked with more attitude than she expected to have.

"During the group today. I noticed that Destiny seems to like you. She has had a hard time in life. It's nice to see her have friends."

"Oh yeah, I guess," Zoey shrugged. "Did you happen to notice my other friend too?"

Dr. Hall chuckled, "Yes. I saw Kelsey. Don't put any blame on her, she's also been through quite a lot. Just try to ignore her. So, have you spoken to your dad yet?"

"Yeah..." Zoey straightened her posture. "So, can we talk about me leaving yet? I need to get back to work."

Dr. Hall gave a half smile. "Listen, Zoey. I want to help you. I know you need to get back to work but I need you to try to relax first. I believe stress is causing a big part of why you may be forgetting some parts of your day."

"Wait... are you telling me that I got so stressed out, I ended up here?" Zoey laughed in disbelief.

"It's possible," Dr. Hall nodded. "Stress can do a lot of things to the body which is why self-care is important. I understand that you need to get back to work but work will always be there. You can always go back."

Zoey ran her hands through her hair and took a deep breath.

"But you're not understanding!"

The frustration in her voice grew. "My clients rely on me... I don't have people that work for me," she paused, "ugh, never mind you won't understand."

"Zoey your health is more important than your clients."

What's important is getting me the hell out of this place...

"Can we please end today's session?" Zoey groaned.

Her chest started to feel heavy and she did not want to begin hyperventilating in front of Dr. Hall again.

"Yes, that's fine. We can pick up tomorrow," Dr. Hall said as she typed on the keyboard of her laptop.

"Can't wait," Zoey muttered and walked out of the office without saying goodbye.

Rather than go to dinner, she went back to her room wishing it was her apartment instead.

CHAPTER 8

DEC 18ᵗʰ

8:30 A.M.

Hunger pains so horrendous, it felt like knives were being dug into Zoey's stomach as soon as she woke up. So, she went straight to the cafeteria just before they stopped serving breakfast and chomped on the scrambled eggs, toast, and sausage links; happy to fill her stomach. The cafeteria nurse had come by with her medication and once again, Zoey hid it when she turned around. She finished her food, happy to have eaten alone, then marched straight to Dr. Hall's office.

I am getting myself out of here today... I can't be kept here any longer!

She knocked rapidly on the door until Dr. Hall opened it.

"Yes, can I help you?"

"Yes, you can," Zoey went to walk in her office, but Dr. Hall stopped her.

"You can't just walk in here."

Zoey sighed impatiently, "Sorry. Can I please come in?"

"I'm busy right now. Is this urgent, Zoey?" Dr. Hall asked.

"When will I be able to leave? How am I doing to you? Are you seeing progress? Can

you give me a sort of time frame or something?"
Zoey asked impatiently.

"I've been here seven days already. I
need-"

"You need to relax your mind, that's what
you need," Dr. Hall interrupted. "It's really up to
you on how much longer you'll be here. If you
slow down and RELAX maybe you will get out of
here sooner than you think... you look tired,
have you been sleeping well?"

Is she kidding?

Zoey looked at Dr. Hall speechless and
turned back down the hallway towards her room.

2:30 P.M.

Zoey sat in front of the computer screen
nearly frozen as she stared at her unread
emails.

*I can't put this off any longer... I have to
say something to them...*

She took a deep breath, clicked on
compose message, and started typing.

Hello,

*Hope all is well. Thank you again for
choosing me to photograph your beautiful
family. I have received your email and I
wanted to very much apologize for not
getting back to you sooner. I am writing to
tell you some unfortunate news about your
photos. I have been in the hospital for a few
days now with no access to my editing
equipment or cell phone. Unfortunately, I do
not think I will gain access to it in time for*

*the holidays which in turn will not allow me
to deliver your photos on time. As an
apology and for your inconvenience, I will be
refunding your money including your deposit
as soon as I am able. I will make sure to send
a confirmation email when I do so. However,
when I do get out of the hospital, I will still
complete your photos and send them to you
free of charge. I, unfortunately, cannot give
you a time frame on that as I just don't know
when that will be. Again, I am deeply sorry
for the inconvenience. Please understand
that this matter is very much out of my
hands. I do understand your frustration and
disappointment with me as I would feel the
same way.*

> *Thank you,*
> *Zoey Martin*

Zoey copied the message and opened
four new message drafts, then pasted what she
had written into each one and sent it to her
clients. She sat back in her chair; eyes fixed on
the screen

*Hopefully, none of you have seen the
video…*

"And now I wait," she sighed.

"Wait for what?" Debra asked.

"Huh?" Zoey had completely forgotten
Debra was sitting next to her until she heard her
speak.

"Oh… uh, for my clients to tell me that
they're never using me again and that I'm going
to go out of business now," she rolled her eyes.

"I see... Well hopefully, that won't happen!" Debra said, innocently.

Hopefully, you're right...

"I have good news for you all!" Dr. Hall suddenly announced at the doorway. "The weather's looking good. We can go outside now!"

"YES!" Lisa jumped happily up and down from across the room.

Everyone else's excitement followed, including Zoey who shocked herself when she smiled.

Dr. Hall led them out of the activity room and down the hallway of where her office was located and stopped in front of a closed door, which Zoey had always thought was just another patient's room. Dr. Hall opened the door, which revealed another door that led out to a set of stairs. They followed her down one level which led to the courtyard and all the patients eagerly walked out in a single file.

When she stepped outside, Zoey took a deep breath of the fresh air and for the first time in a week, she did not feel trapped. She looked at the other patients who were aimlessly walking around the yard, dancing to the music that Debra played from her portable speakers while others did yoga in the grass. Tina and Lisa started to do cartwheels and Destiny acted out a ballet dance near the garden. Will dribbled a basketball onto the sidewalk and dunked it into an imaginary net.

Zoey went to the corner of the courtyard and sat cross-legged in the grass with her back rested against the fence. She continued to watch all the patients that she's been surrounded by for the past week and began to wonder what really led them to be in the hospital. She looked up to the sky, then closed her eyes.

Am I ever really going to remember what happened to me?

4:30 P.M.

After examining the photo of the Davis family for the past half an hour, Zoey spotted something odd on top of the star on the tree.

"Oh, wait a second..." she gasped as she could suddenly recall the sound of the star falling and the daughter apologizing profusely.

"Dr. Davis glued it back together... I remember that now..."

Zoey hysterically turned to a new page of her notebook as she sat on her bed and began writing.

"I had the daughter stand on the ladder and put the star on the tree for a photo. She dropped it and it broke... I remember that now. Mrs. Davis got mad... then that's when she went to throw up. Dr. Davis fixed the star and we ended up getting the shot... but-- but what else happened after that? I didn't go to the police til the middle of the night... my shoot was in the daytime."

Zoey rubbed her head wishing that it would make her confusion go away. In an attempt to distract herself, she took a shower and then headed to Dr. Hall's office for her session.

5:00 P.M.

"Did you enjoy being outside today?" Dr. Hall asked.

"It was fine," Zoey shrugged.

"I saw you smiling. That was nice to see," Dr. Hall remarked.

"Yup. I guess," Zoey shifted uncomfortably in her seat.

"You don't seem as happy right now, though."

How can I be happy when I'm sitting here, and not at home?

"I don't know what to tell you," Zoey sighed. "I just really want to get back home, and I know you're not going to allow me out of here anytime soon so… I am just trying to make the best of this situation. Anyway, I contacted my clients like you suggested."

Dr. Hall typed something on her laptop, then turned her attention back to Zoey.

"Good. Were you honest with them?" she asked.

"Yeah. I told them that I'm in the hospital and can't deliver their photos in time, so I'm refunding everybody," Zoey winced as she said the word *refund*.

"It's okay, you'll make that money back. Your health is what's important right now," Dr. Hall said.

How do you expect me to make thousands of dollars back that easily?

"So Zoey, to answer your question about progress earlier," she continued, "I do think you are progressing just a bit... but that doesn't mean you are ready to leave. You still have a way to go."

Zoey's eyes felt like they were going to pop out of her head. "Wait, what? What are you talking about? A long way?" she stuttered, "but, I'm remembering things. I remember getting handcuffed and part of the photoshoot now. Isn't that enough? How much longer do I need to be here? I mean, I really do not belong here. I JUST forgot some stuff for a day, that's it..."

Dr. Hall gave her a serious look. "Can you remember why you thought you saw your mom yet?"

This woman is going to make me pull my hair out.

"No. I. Cannot. Remember that," Zoey said with clenched fists.

Dr. Hall crossed her arms as if she were waiting for Zoey to keep speaking but instead, Zoey stared back without saying a word.

After a few seconds of silence, Dr. Hall was the first to talk. "I know you're frustrated but you are doing good. You just need to work on your anger and anxiety, Zoey. Let the rest of your memories come back on their own. If you want to go home; first I need to make sure that you are well enough to be by yourself and I don't think you are quite there yet. Okay?"

I'm never getting out of here...

Zoey nodded as she had barely any will to argue anymore.

"Is there anything else on your mind that you'd like to talk about with me today?" Dr. Hall asked.

"I have nothing else to say to you," Zoey muttered, got up from her chair and walked back to her room, wiping her tears along the way.

CHAPTER 9

DEC 19th

6:00 A.M.

Zoey immediately started to panic when she woke up and the first thing that she thought of was emailing her client's the day before.

Everything is going to be fine. I will figure all this out and my life will go back to normal... I just need to distract myself right now...

Since the cafeteria did not open for another hour, Zoey decided to do yoga to not only ease her mind but make time pass by faster.

She sat on the floor, then laid on her back and raised her hips into a bridge, held it for ten seconds, dropped back down and repeated the movement five more times before turning onto her stomach. She arched herself back, using her hands to hold herself up while she dropped her head back- eye line to the ceiling. She then moved into the downward dog position and repeated these movements until she lost the strength to hold herself up. She stood up and inhaled deep while reaching her arms and head towards the ceiling, then exhaled as she dropped them both to her feet, keeping her legs straight and back bent over. After hanging there for a few seconds, Zoey straightened back up and closed her eyes, counted to thirty, and then looked directly at the clock.

Seriously…

She was disappointed to see that only ten minutes had passed by and without even thinking about it, she pulled off her socks, opened the door of her room, and bolted out into a fast run.

She ran down the hallway and rounded the corner, passing Derek's room just as Tee was walking by.

"No running!" he shouted.

Zoey turned around, now jogging in place. "I'm not running. I'm jogging. It helps with my anxiety… you should mark that in my chart."

Tee raised an eyebrow. "Don't run into anyone and ONLY keep it at a jog."

"Eye, eye captain," Zoey saluted him.

She continued down the hallway, slowing her pace where she spotted Miriam ahead of her. "Morning, Miriam," she said.

Miriam nodded, "yup another hellish mornin' here."

"Ain't that the truth," Zoey muttered and continued down the hall.

She looped around the whole floor six times before Kelsey woke up and opened her door. Having half a thought to mess with her, Zoey reverted her route and jogged back to her room.

Out of breath and drenched in sweat, she took a fast shower, changed into a black pair of leggings and a hoodie, then went to the cafeteria.

When she got there, the cafeteria nurse walked right up to her as soon as she sat down and asked if she wanted her medication now or later.

I hate this so much.

Zoey took the pill and acted like she swallowed, then shoved it in her hoodie pocket when the nurse turned away.

"UGH!" Destiny sighed loudly as she fiddled with her food.

"What's wrong Destiny? You look sad today," Zoey remarked.

Destiny's eyes started to become teary. "I really like Will. Why won't he like me? I don't get him. He's such a mystery," she sniffled, then turned around to look towards his direction.

He was sitting alone at a table in the farthest side of the room.

"I don't think it's you, Destiny. I think it's him," Zoey tried to reassure her.

"Yeah, I mean look at him. He's always alone. I wouldn't be surprised if he tried to kill someone before," Tina who was sitting across from her, added in a whisper.

I was thinking the same thing...

"Well, I don't care what he's done. I like him and I want him to like me," Destiny said displeased. "I'm trying again."

She jumped up from the table and walked towards Will.

Zoey watched her strut over and plop herself right next to him as she began twirling her curls.

"I wonder if he even knows that she's there," Tina shook her head.

"Excuse me, everyone. I have a surprise!" the cafeteria nurse announced by the door. "Come with me if you'd like to see."

Great more surprises.

"What about our food? We're not done eating!" Derek called out.

"Just leave it at your table, you can finish when we're done," the nurse said.

Everyone in the cafeteria, including Zoey followed her to the activity room. When she opened the door to it, Lisa gasped as she was the first to see the fake Christmas tree in the middle of the room.

"Why isn't it decorated?" Destiny crossed her arms.

"That's part of the other surprise," Dr. Hall said as she went to stand next to the tree. "You get to take turns decorating. There are some decorations in those boxes over here." She pointed to three large cardboard boxes filled with holiday decorations next to the tree. "You can all decorate the tree with whatever is in them."

Lisa smiled ear to ear as she jumped around with her doll.

"Can we start now?" she asked giddily.

"Sure, go ahead," Dr. Hall nodded, and Lisa immediately went for one of the boxes.

Tina followed, along with Destiny who asked Will to join but he harshly declined and walked away.

She flipped her hair and cleared her throat. "Well then, I guess I'll decorate without you."

"Zoey, are you gonna help?" Tina asked, holding a handful of Christmas lights.

"Uh… may--maybe…" Zoey stuttered as she stood in a trance.

It's about to be Christmas… and I'm celebrating it in a mental hospital… a behavioral center, psych ward… a hospital... a whatever the hell this place is…

She looked at the patients who were dressing the tree with lights while throwing tinsel at each other and suddenly, she burst out into a hysterical laugh. Nothing was making any sense to her anymore.

Zoey fell to her knees in an uncontrollable continuous laugh. "I can't believe I'm still here... oh my god, I'm really here..." she gasped in between laughs.

"OOOOH, she's doing a joker impression!" Kelsey pointed at her and laughed too.

After a good minute, Zoey finally began to stop herself. She sat up from rolling on the floor. "I'm sorry, I'm sorry," she said to the girls, trying to keep her composure. "I'm not laughing at you, I'm just-"

"-it's okay," Destiny shrugged. "It happens all the time. No biggie. We all have our breakdowns, even Derek." She elbowed him on his right side, "Right Derek?"

He flinched and dropped a handful of string lights, then covered himself with his arms, as if he were naked.

"Why are you touching us?" he gasped.

"What? You don't like being touched?" Destiny poked at his side and chuckled.

"AH, get away from me!" he yelled and then darted out of the room still covering himself.

"Nice one," Tina laughed.

This is my new life...

Zoey knelt in front of one of the boxes and pulled out a small, crafted angel ornament. As she held it, the memory of painting Christmas ornaments with her mom when she was a kid, just like the one in her hand came back to her. Staring at the angel and the tree in front of her made Zoey think back to those days of Christmas decorating with her family; the days she would look forward to as a child. It wasn't until now that she had not realized the last time that she decorated a Christmas tree was over ten years ago.

"Now Tina's the tree!" Lisa's voice broke Zoey out of her thoughts and she looked up from the angel to see the girls dressing Tina up in Tinsel and lights. Christmas music sounded from the computer courtesy of DJ Debra.

Deep breaths... Deep breaths...

Zoey crawled herself back against the wall, still holding the angel. She watched the girls play with the tinsel which reminded her of the tinsel fights she had with her mom while her dad strung lights around the tree.

She gazed at the Christmas tree in front of her now and pictured her dad topping it off with the angel while her mother would panic that he would fall off the ladder.

Like Mrs. Davis freaked out on Dr. Davis...

Suddenly, something plastic hit the side of Zoey's head, distracting her from her thoughts. It was a shiny red ball ornament that Lisa threw at her.

"Come on! You'll have fun decorating!" she urged.

Zoey picked the ball up and stared at her reflection through it.

Might as well.

10:18 A.M.

After staring at the photo again in her room for over an hour, Zoey's eyes caught attention to the scar on Mrs. Davis's chest... and her eyes widened as she realized what her scar was.

"You have cancer... I remember now. That's why that scar is reminding me of my mom... I have to write this down..."

Zoey fumbled for her notebook under her blanket and wrote down her new fact about Mrs. Davis, then started pacing in the room.

"How could I have forgotten about that family? They reminded me so much of mine..."

She smacked her forehead with the palm of her right hand.

Although Zoey was relieved to remember, she felt stupid that she had even forgotten about the Davis family in the first place.

I left right after she threw up... I was only there for two hours. The shoot was supposed to start at 1:00 but I was late... I must have left by at least 4:00 or 5:00 at the latest...

"But where did I go after?" she thought out loud.

"I don't know where you went but lunch is being served early today if you're hungry," Tee interrupted. He stood at the door with his arms crossed.

"I didn't even hear you open the door. You're like a mouse," Zoey sighed.

"I appreciate that," he grinned and walked away, leaving the door open.

I can't wait to get my privacy back...

The sound of Zoey's stomach rumbling started to distract her from her thoughts. Resisting the urge to keep staring at the photo, she took her notebook and then went to the cafeteria to quickly eat and hurry back to her room.

11:30 A.M.

Zoey took a bite of her grilled cheese sandwich and immediately spit it out onto her plate. She began to stand up to go throw it away but stopped herself when she spotted the cafeteria nurse in the corner. She had a tablet in her hand, and she was staring right at Zoey.

She's probably taking notes on everything I do... Which is why I should look as normal as possible.

Zoey sat back down. "Because I am," she muttered and reluctantly picked the sandwich back up and took a few more bites, trying not to gag.

"Hey, Zo Zo!" Destiny skipped over towards her. "Ew, you're eating that?"

She poked at Zoey's sandwich. "These sandwiches are nasty. Don't they taste like cardboard?"

"Actually, yes. Yes, they do," Zoey nodded, "but the nurse was eyeing me down, so I figured I'd eat it. I want Dr. Hall to know that I'm not," she paused before finishing the sentence with the word *crazy*, "I just want Dr. Hall to know that I'm actually trying here."

Destiny sat down in front of her. "I see. So, I'm surprised Dr. Grinch got a tree for us."

"Right," Zoey stood up with her tray, "well, I'm going to go back to my room so…"

"Wait!" Destiny stopped her. "Want to see my princess drawings?"

"Uh, no… that's okay," Zoey said, trying to not hurt Destiny's feelings. "I started remembering some stuff. I kind of want to go back to my room to figure it all out more."

"Ooooh, maybe I can help," Destiny clapped. "I love a good mystery!"

At this point, I guess I'll try anything.

Zoey sat back down and pulled her notebook out of her hoodie pocket to show Destiny.

"Okay, so I remember being at my photoshoot and sort of being at the police station now… I just don't remember what happened before it or after it."

Destiny flipped through her notes.

"And your aaaaabsolutely for sure - for sure positive, that you didn't take any drugs?" she asked as she looked at her oddly.

Why did I think this girl would be of any help to me?

Zoey rolled her eyes and shook her head, no.

Destiny set aside the book after combing through the rest of the pages.

"Hmm, this is so weird. I've never met anyone with a missing memory of just one day ONLY. Very intriguing of you, Zo Zo!" She nodded her head in approval.

"Yeah, I guess I am pretty interesting, huh," Zoey sighed.

"Don't worry, Zo Zo. We'll escape this godforsaken dungeon one day."

Will we, though?

2:00 P.M.

After typing her username and password to her email account, Zoey hovered the cursor over the login button and closed her eyes.

"Whatever happens, happens. It's done already. I can't take it back now."

She inhaled deep and clicked, still keeping her eyes shut.

One, two, three.

She slowly exhaled, opened one eye, and then the other. There were four new unread emails, all from her clients.

"You got this," Debra smiled with a thumbs up.

Easy for you to say.

"Thanks," Zoey sneered.

She opened the first email, which was from Mrs. Gonzalez.

Hello Zoey, I am so sorry to hear that. I hope you get better soon! I understand that the situation is out of your hands. Yes,

158

please notify me once my refund goes through. I do look forward to seeing the photos whenever possible, as well. Hang in there!

Okay, not too bad. She seems… understanding. Let's see what Mrs. Vanetti says…

Hi Zoey, thank you for contacting me. I'm sorry to hear about your situation and I understand that you're tied up, but would you happen to have someone who could send me my refund sooner? I'd like to use that money for another photographer if I can find one this late. I am very disappointed in hearing this. Thank you.

And I'm just as disappointed as you are, Mrs. Vanetti. Okay, next…

Thank you for contacting me with the update. I saw your video and am praying for your recovery. Take care. - Kerry Garcia

Of course, a client would see it… I can't think about that right now.
Zoey clicked on to the next email, and her heart felt like it had fallen to her feet once she saw that it was from Dr. Davis.
I told him I was visiting a friend in the hospital, then I emailed him and said that I'm the one in the hospital… I look so dumb.
Sighing, Zoey opened the email. It read

Afternoon Zoey, thank you for contacting me. I understand and will await the photos when you are ready. Please take care of yourself and Happy Holidays.

"Yeah, Happy Freaking Holidays," Zoey groaned.

"That's the spirit!" Debra said cheerfully.

Ignoring her, Zoey logged off without replying to anyone and stood up from her chair.

"Zo Zo! We're doing Christmas crafts. Want to join?" Destiny called out from the table when she saw Zoey stand up.

"I'm not really an artsy person..." Zoey said.

"Well no one is that great of an artist as I am," Destiny laughed, "But that's okay! You can still try. We're painting decorations, come on!"

Zoey looked at the clock on the wall, which showed that only half an hour of activity time had gone by. If she wanted to look like she was trying, then Zoey knew she had to stay there for at least another half hour.

"Fine, I guess I'll decorate," she groaned and went over to sit in the open space between Destiny and Derek who was hunched over the table, painting a hand-sized wooden tree. Destiny gave Zoey a five by seven wood picture frame; the kind you find in the children's arts and crafts section of a store.

"Here Zo Zo. It's a picture frame to paint! You like taking pictures, you can paint this for one of your photos!" she cheered.

"Oh wow, that's really nice of you... Thanks, Destiny," Zoey said, surprised.

Guess this girl isn't so bad…

Zoey spent the rest of the half-hour painting the frame in black and red diagonal stripes. When she was done, she chose a small Christmas wreath from the pile of ornaments and painted it in green and red. It did not hit her until after she was done painting, that she decorated the little wreath almost identical to the one she had painted when she was eight. It made her think back to her mother, hanging that wreath up on their front door every Christmas after.

The memory of the wreath caused tears to sneak out of Zoey's eyes and she wiped them away as soon as she felt them drop down her cheeks.

Destiny noticed and patted her back.

"Debra said we can keep our crafts to decorate our rooms if we want," she said.

Why am I suddenly so emotional all the time? I can't keep letting this happen…

Zoey stood up with the wreath and the picture frame.

"Thanks… I'm tired. I'm going to go back to my room. I'll see you later Destiny," she sniffled.

Zoey left the activity room and rushed down the hall as she fought off another panic attack.

5:00 P.M.

"Let's talk about the things you did in the few days before you got here," Dr. Hall said. "Do

161

you remember anything you did during that time?"

Is she serious?

"Uh, yeah... I just don't remember what I did on the tenth, well part of the tenth. I remember being at the photoshoot now, but nothing after," Zoey paused, "yet."

"Okay, tell me anything you can remember during that week," Dr. Hall said as she opened her laptop.

She is serious... deep breaths...

Zoey sat up in her chair. "The day before I had a photoshoot in the evening. It was a family of over ten people and the shoot went late. The days before that were regular, I guess... I had a few photoshoots scheduled at different times, did my workouts, went about my day really," she shrugged.

"How were you feeling on those days?" Dr. Hall asked.

"Um, fine I guess," Zoey paused, "tired... but that was because of all the editing. The shoots aren't what's tiring. It's the editing process that can sometimes take days to finish."

Which is what I should be doing right now.

Dr. Hall tapped her fingers against the keyboard, quickly.

"So that can be kind of stressful, I can imagine?" she asked.

Here she goes again.

"Well, yeah... but that's my job. Any job is stressful," Zoey said.

"What kind of editing do you do? I know nothing about photography. I just enjoy looking at nice photos," Dr. Hall chuckled.

"Most people do," Zoey muttered. "Well, it depends. I retouch skin, fix stray hairs or get rid of ugly backgrounds: things like tacky wall outlets, wardrobe malfunctions," she paused, "broken stars… like the one at Dr. Davis's house."

"Oh yeah? What happened with the broken star?" Dr. Hall asked.

"I remember it falling during the shoot, which made me remember Mrs. Davis getting mad about it and then getting sick. Then I left their house shortly after. I remembered all this after I stared at the photo about a million time-"

Out of the blue, rain began to pound heavily against the office window, followed by the sound of thunder causing the lights in the office to flicker, and it distracted Zoey from finishing her sentence. She unknowingly, gripped on to the arms of her chair as she suddenly thought of sitting in her own apartment watching the rain through the window.

"Are you okay?" Dr. Hall asked as she reached her hand out to Zoey.

"Uh, I think. I, I don't know… the lights just now… they flickered, and I thought of my apartment for some reason… I don't know… it distracted me. It was like Déjà vu or something…" Zoey rubbed her head and slumped down in her chair.

"How have you been feeling on the medication I gave you? Has it helped with your anxiety at all?" Dr. Hall asked.

Not one bit.

"Yeah, it's helped," Zoey lied.

"Good!" Dr. Hall said as she typed.

Zoey leaned in closer to the desk, tilting her head to try to read the laptop screen. But unfortunately, from its position, she had no luck. "What are you typing?!" she demanded.

"I'm not writing bad things. I'm just keeping some notes about you as I've told you that before," Dr. Hall said reassuringly. "I can tell that you are frustrated, Zoey. I'm going to prescribe you another medication to deal with your anger outbursts."

OH MY GOD... THIS LADY IS REALLY ABOUT TO SEE AN ANGER OUTBURST.

"Anger outbursts?!" Zoey swallowed, "you realize why I'm angry, right? I'm scared. I don't remember what I did but that doesn't mean I belong here... I'm not like Derek. I'm not like Destiny. I'm not bipolar. I don't have schizophrenia like Kelsey does," she stuttered. "I, I just lost my memory for a day! Wouldn't you feel the same if you were me?"

She wiped away the tears that were now flowing from her eyes.

"Great, now I'm crying. Thanks," Zoey huffed.

"I'm sorry this happened to you. I would probably feel the same way if I was in your situation but the more you get frustrated, the less your answers will come." Dr. Hall leaned into her desk, "You are a hard-working woman and I think that is great. You have priorities, you care about your work, but I need you to focus MORE on yourself. You need to do things that

164

make you happy. The brain works in mysterious ways. Stress is a big factor on the brain. It can cause you to lose sight of reality sometimes. It can even cause you to forget. Just like traumatic events cause the same thing... and you have been through a traumatic event before as well."

"If you're talking about my mom dying, that happened ten years ago... why would that cause me to forget a random day all of a sudden?" Zoey scrunched her forehead in confusion.

"I also mentioned stress. Zoey, you just need a little bit of patience. You ARE progressing," Dr. Hall said.

"If I'm progressing, then why are you prescribing me more medication?" Zoey questioned.

Dr. Hall looked at her sincerely. "You know what, I'm going to keep you on the same medication... for now."

"Okay bu-- but how much more do I need to progress to leave?" Zoey stuttered.

"Just a little more patience and I think you will get there. Remember, try to use this time to try to really focus on yourself while you are here. I have another session in half an hour and a conference call in between. Do you mind if we cut this session short or would you like to talk about anything else with me today?"

I'd like to talk about me leaving TODAY.

"No, it's okay. I'll see you tomorrow," Zoey sighed.

She walked out of the office, squeezing her fists so tight that she left nail marks in the skin of her palms.

CHAPTER 10

DEC 20th

5:00 A.M.

The sound of the rain hitting against the window weakened as it began lightening up and Zoey watched it now drop to a drizzle. Her body was shaking as the anxiety in her grew.

"I need to control myself. Don't cry… Don't cry," she told herself as she tried holding back tears. "I need to get out of here… I need to go for a walk or something… I need to distract myself." She pushed her chair back from the computer and walked out of the room. The tears began to flow as she rushed through the hall to go outside.

"Stop crying!" she smacked herself on the cheek.

Why can't I get out of this mood? Why!

Zoey stepped outside but just as she did so, the rain began to fall and within the next minute, she was standing under a downpour.

"Ugh fine, I'll just go back inside then!" she muttered and went to turn around, but something caught her eye. She squinted to see off into the distance.

"That can't be…"

She took a few steps closer.

"MOM? MOM? WAIT! WAIT FOR ME!"

Zoey began to run towards her in the pouring rain as thunder shook the sky.

"I SEE YOU!! WAIT WAIT!!!"

"Zoey, honey! Zoey!"

"I'm here, I'm here," Zoey called out.

"Everything's going to be okay, it's okay."

She reached out for her mom's hand but couldn't grab it.

"Wait, wait for me!" she called out again, but her mother disappeared around the corner and Zoey was left alone in the pouring rain.

"Wake up, honey," Debra's voice suddenly jolted Zoey awake, and she woke up gasping for air.

"It's okay, calm down. You were dreaming again. Here, take this," Debra held out a small pill in the palm of her hand.

"Wh-- what time is it?" Zoey stuttered as she sat up.

"It's five in the morning," Debra said. "Here, please take this. Just try to go back to sleep for a little while longer, at least until breakfast opens."

Zoey reluctantly grabbed the pill, put it in her mouth, and acted as if she swallowed.

"Open," Debra said.

Now, all of a sudden, I can't be trusted?

Zoey didn't know what else to do so she swallowed the pill and opened her mouth. Debra made her lift her tongue, then reminded her that she was just around the corner if she needed anything, before walking out of the room. When she left, Zoey immediately grabbed her notebook off the nightstand and began writing.

DECEMBER 20th - DREAMT OF SITTING IN FRONT OF MY COMPUTER AT HOME. IT WAS POURING, I WAS GETTING FRUSTRATED, I WENT FOR A WALK, MOM WAS THERE.

The medicine that Debra gave Zoey started to kick in and she was becoming so dizzy, it was hard to focus on the paper. She closed her eyes and fell right back to sleep, minutes later.

8:30 A.M.

"AHHH!! They're coming for us! I've been warning you!" Zoey awoke to the sound of Derek shrieking from his room.

"Shut up!" someone yelled from another room.

Why is this happening to me?

Zoey threw her blanket to the ground, leaped out of the bed in aggravation, then marched out of her room and down the hallway towards Derek's.

His door was open when she got there, so she stomped right in.

"Excuse you! I was sleeping! I'd appreciate not waking up to hearing your bloody murder screams!" Zoey nearly growled.

Derek, who had stopped screaming as soon as she walked in, huddled in the corner of his bed and pulled his knees to his chest like a scared child. Zoey took a step closer to him.

"So, if you're going to scream, then close your door before you do it! OKAY?"

"AHHHH!" Derek busted out into a loud scream as tears began to fall down his face.

"Are you kidding me?" Zoey huffed.

She walked out of the room, immensely aggravated and headed to get her breakfast.

"I need to get out of here. I need to get out of here. I will get myself out... I will... I will," she repeated to herself as she headed to the cafeteria.

When she got there, the cafeteria lady gave Zoey the last of the cold scrambled eggs and hash browns, then she went to sit with Lisa, Tina, and Destiny who were already sitting together at a table. As soon as she sat down, the nurse walked right up to her and Zoey held her palm out.

"This is becoming routine, you know?" she smirked.

The nurse didn't say anything and instead, dropped the pill into her hand.

Zoey took it, then spit it out and hid it as soon as she walked away.

"Why do you even take it if you're not actually TAKING it?" Lisa asked.

"I want them to think I'm taking the medication, so it looks like I'm progressing," Zoey air quoted. "But don't tell anyone..."

Lisa swiped a finger over her mouth. "Mums the word Zoey! I won't tell, shh," she giggled.

Let's hope not.

Zoey picked up the runny eggs with her fork and took a bite.

"I don't even know why I grabbed this," she groaned.

"Ew, it looks disgusting," Tina commented.

Zoey spit out the egg onto her plate and nodded, "yup… that's because it is."

She wiped her mouth with a napkin and pushed the plate away.

"Well, I still would've been sleeping if it wasn't for Derek and the hundred other people inside of him."

"Oh yeah, I heard him screaming too. Thank god I'm not in the same hallway as that psycho," Destiny laughed. She looked at Zoey and made an awkward face, "oh sorry."

"Yeah… thanks," Zoey sighed. She dropped her forehead on the lunch table.

Destiny slid closer. "You okay, Zo Zo?"

I really, really hate that name.

Zoey lifted her head. "No, I'm not okay. I'm tired… I'm confused… I want to go home. Ugh! I had another dream this morning, but Debra woke me up before it ended, and then she gave me something that knocked me out. Now I can't really remember anything. I wrote it down, but I still don't get it…"

"We'll figure it out, Zo Zo," Destiny patted her back.

WE don't need to figure it out, I DO.

Zoey dropped her head back down on to the table.

11:15 A.M.

The brain works in mysterious ways…

Dr. Hall's words repeated in Zoey's mind while she sat on her bed, trapped in her thoughts.

If stress can cause memory loss, then why haven't I lost my memory before? I've been WAY more stressed than this...

The feeling of anxiety started to soar throughout Zoey's body. So, she got off the bed, took off her socks, threw her arms into the air in a V shape, and inhaled deeply as she bent over to reach her ankles. She exhaled and dropped down into a runner's stretch and counted out loud.

"One, two, three!"

She shot up from the floor, opened the door of her room, and darted down the hallway.

Gaining speed, she spotted Derek standing outside of his door directly in her way.

"Out of the way, Derek!" she warned.

When he saw her, he dove into his room just in time and Zoey chuckled to herself as she rounded the corner, light on her feet. As she ran, she began to forget that she was in the hospital. The hallways turned into the sidewalks of the city and she could feel the light breeze on her face while the sun beat down on her skin.

"Woah! No running!" Tee shouted just before she almost ran right into his shoulder.

He grabbed her by the arms to stabilize her from falling.

"Uh, sorry I was jogging again," Zoey said through deep breaths.

"JOGGING is fine. Not running," he scolded.

"Right, sorry. I'm done," she put up her hand innocently.

"Last warning," he raised his eyebrow and continued walking.

Zoey stood there in the middle of the hallway, hands on her knees, breathing heavily.

"You were running so fast, if Tee didn't catch you, you would've fallen straight to the floor! How did you not see him?" Destiny asked and Zoey gasped as she heard Destiny speak.

"Oh god, you scared me Destiny... Where did you even come from? You just... appeared."

"Oops," Destiny shrugged, not answering her. "Ew, you're all sweaty now, Zo Zo. That's not very attractive."

Zoey rolled her eyes. "Yeah, I know. I'll shower later. I'm going to go get lunch first. I'm starving."

Destiny perked up and clapped her hands, excitedly.

"Oh, lunch! Yay let's go!" she squealed and skipped down the hall towards the cafeteria.

That wasn't an invitation but sure, let's go.

1:00 P.M.

"Hey, sorry I didn't call you back. I worked a double for the past two days. How are you feeling?" Alex asked as soon as Zoey called her.

"I'm feeling sick of that question. I'm aggravated, tired, annoyed. I just want to go home! I can't believe it's been over a week already. Christmas is literally in five days..." Zoey vented.

173

"Have you remembered anything else yet?" Alex asked.

After Zoey took a few minutes to briefly explain what she could remember, Alex summed up, "so the part that your still forgetting is what happened between you leaving the shoot and arriving at the police station."

"Yeah..." Zoey hesitated, "I feel so confused. When I was running down the hallway earlier, I literally felt like I was outside. It was like my brain made me think that I wasn't in the hospital anymore... until I ran into Tee. It's all a blur... Dr. Hall told me that she thinks I'm too stressed and that may be the cause of my memory loss."

"Stress can cause memory loss?" Alex asked. She sounded as skeptical as Zoey had when she first heard it.

"Apparently, yes. I asked the same thing. I just don't see how regular stress could have made me think my mom came back to life... It doesn't make any sense. She also told me that traumatic events cause memory loss too but the only traumatic thing I've gone through is my mom dying and that-"

"-was ten years ago," Alex finished her sentence. "You know," she paused, "the holidays are normally rough for you, and you did have some Christmas shoots..."

She makes a point...

"Oh, which speaking of Christmas shoots, I forgot to tell you; I remember why Mrs. Davis was sick now. The more I looked at the photo, I noticed her scar and I kept thinking about my mom having one... Then I realized that Dr.

Davis told me that she had cancer when she got sick on the shoot."

"Uh, sis… I think that may have something to do with you forgetting the rest of your day," Alex said in a sincere voice.

"Eh, yeah… maybe," Zoey was hesitant to believe it was true, "but I remember the photoshoot. I got through it with no problem… nothing bad happened… except Mrs. Davis being sick… and even if that has something to do with me thinking my mom was alive, I didn't go to the police until after midnight. My shoot was in the afternoon… I couldn't have been there past 4 or 5 o'clock, the latest. Ugh, this is so aggravating."

Every time Zoey thought about Monday, she became more confused and irritated. All she wanted to do was go home.

"Have you told the Doctor any of this?" Alex asked.

"Yeah, but I don't think she cares too much about me remembering anything… I think she only cares more about me not acting crazy again. She normally asks things about my family and my personal life, which has made her think that all I do is work. She keeps telling me to relax but that's literally impossible here."

"Well, you do kind of work a lot… but you have to," Alex said.

"Exactly. I was trying to explain that to her. I just can't see how stress led me here. I can't accept it until I remember the whole day… I mean, I literally saw my mom die in front of me a whole decade ago. There is just no way I would have thought that she's alive. I haven't been that stressed lately... It doesn't make any sense..."

The amount of confusion, Zoey felt was beginning to equally irritate and scare her at the same time.

"Don't get discouraged. You have remembered a lot so far from what you told me... You're just missing a little bit more. We will figure it out, sis. I'll come by after work tonight," Alex reassured her.

Zoey could tell that Alex was just as confused and worried as she was. However, she was doing her best to keep it together, mainly for Zoey's sake. They said goodbye to each other, and Zoey hung up the phone, then went to the activity room.

Just as she entered, Dr. Hall walked in behind her, dragging a large container nearly half the size of Zoey.

"I have a surprise for everyone!" Dr. Hall happily announced as she went to stand next to the tree.

This place is just full of surprises...

Everyone eagerly gathered around Dr. Hall except for Zoey.

Destiny elbowed her. "Come on. It's a good surprise... I promise, Zo Zo!"

Nothing about this place is good...

"We were blessed enough to receive a box full of donated gifts for everyone this year!" Dr. Hall exclaimed.

She waited a moment while the patients shouted in variations of excitement.

"Now, I'm going to go through them one at a time. You each get one gift only,"

Dr. Hall continued as she reached in and pulled out the first gift. "I have some brand-new lip gloss sets here. I bet I know who wants-"

"-ME, ME!" Destiny raised her hand.

"Ah, I knew it," Dr. Hall smiled and handed it to her.

"Is there more makeup?!" Lisa pouted.

"Let's see, Lisa," Dr. Hall fumbled around the box before pulling out a clown wig in one hand and a doll dressed in a blue nightgown decorated by yellow stars, in the other.

"Never mind makeup!" Lisa gasped, "can I have the doll, please? PLEASE!"

"I'll take the wig," Derek said with wide eyes.

Dr. Hall handed Lisa the doll and Derek the wig.

"Oh Zoey, I think you should have this one," she said as she pulled out a small instant polaroid camera from the box. "I bet it's not as fancy as the one you're used to using but it came with some extra film. Here, I bet you know how to work it better than I do!"

She passed the camera to Zoey. It was an older model, probably worth not more than forty dollars and already had a film cartridge with ten photos inside. The bag had two sets of film which contained twenty photos each.

"Thanks," Zoey half-smiled.

Dr. Hall continued to go through the rest of the presents, pulling out more items from shoes, crafts, children's toys to clothes, and more, then dispersed them to the patients.

"Ladies, would you like to do makeovers with me? I haven't put makeup on in foreverrr!

Ugh," Destiny whined, drawing out the ever in her voice.

"I do! We can put some on my baby and her new friend too!" Lisa jumped up and down as she held both dolls in her arms."

"Maybe, Lisa. We'll see about that..." Destiny rolled her eyes and put her hands on her hips. She looked at Zoey.

"Zo Zo, are you in? I can fix those nasty dark bags under your eyes," she said as she batted her eyes and smiled.

It's not even worth being offended.

Zoey smirked, "sure, I'm in."

4:00 P.M.

Gripping onto the sink in front of the mirror, Zoey stared at her bright red lips and green eyeshadow, courtesy of Destiny.

Now I'm playing dress-up...

She went to turn on the water in the shower, but nothing came out. She tried turning the nozzle on and off a few more times, but still no water.

Deep breaths...

Telling herself to stay calm, Zoey stomped out of her room and headed towards the nurse's station.

When she got there, she tapped impatiently on the glass.

"Excuse me! My shower stopped working!"

The nurse behind the glass looked up at her and smiled.

"I'm sorry, just give me a moment," she said before dialing on the phone. She explained the shower issue to whoever was on the other line, then turned her attention back to Zoey. "I'm sorry but no one can come out to fix it right now. You'll have to use another patients shower until they get it fixed. That room has had some issues in the past. It happens sometimes."

Just my luck.

"Fine," Zoey mumbled and went back to her room to quickly grab her clothes, a towel, soap, and shampoo from her bathroom.

Trying not to drop everything in her hands, she headed towards Destiny's room.

"Hey, can I come in? It's Zoey," she called out as she fumbled to knock on her door.

"Come in Zo Zo!" Destiny sang out, clearly in a good mood.

Zoey opened the door and found Destiny standing in front of the mirror, applying more makeup.

"Girl, the look I gave you, made you look so much prettier! Told you, I'd get those nasty bags to disappear!" Destiny said.

"Yeah... uh, can I use your shower? Mine stopped working. I need to wash my hair. It's been a few days as you can tell," Zoey said as she pulled a strand of her greasy thin hair.

"Yeah... I was gonna suggest that you wash that thing soon," Destiny laughed.

"So... can I take a quick shower please?" Zoey asked, trying to stay patient.

Destiny finished applying her mascara and put the wand back in its place. "All yours!" she clapped.

Zoey walked into the bathroom and turned to lock the door behind her on instinct. But of course, Destiny's door had no lock on it either.

I hate this place. I hate this place. I hate this place.

5:00 P.M.

"Good afternoon, Zoey take a seat. How are you feeling today?" Dr. Hall asked as she put away a book on one of the bookshelves in her office.

Zoey sat upright and shifted in her seat. Tears started to stream down her face.

"Honestly, it's killing me that I can't fully remember a whole day... I can't believe I blacked out and ended up here... That's never even happened to me when I've been drunk. "

"I know you are scared... and I know you want to remember but I don't think you should be focusing too much on that," Dr. Hall said. "Being emotional is okay. It's an emotional time for you. It's okay to cry."

"Yeah, it's okay to cry but not right now... I can't get emotional," Zoey argued as the tears kept flowing. "I... I just hate crying. I hate being emotional. I've been an emotional wreck since I got here. This never happens."

Dr. Hall looked Zoey right in the eyes while she clasped her hands together on the desk.

"Zoey I think you were a bit of an emotional wreck right before you came to the hospital. You are on the right path, just try to take it easy. Remember, you can always tell me how you are feeling and what's on your mind. There's no right or wrong answer in this room."

Zoey wiped away her tears and eased her breathing, "Okay. Th-- thank you."

"Zoey, why don't we end our session a little earlier today and you go back to your room and mess with that camera you got. Try to ease your mind from the tenth, just for a little bit," Dr. Hall suggested.

Zoey looked around the room and hesitated before speaking. "I-- I feel like... I feel like... if I don't think about the tenth, then I'll never remember anything at all and then I'm going to be stuck in this hospital forever," she paused and looked at Dr. Hall, "no offense."

"None taken," Dr. Hall smiled. "Just for the remainder of the evening, try to take my advice. See if it will help you. If it doesn't, then at least you can say you tried, right?"

"I guess," Zoey mumbled.

She got up from her chair, left Dr. Hall's office and hurried back to her room.

8:00 P.M.

"I stopped at your apartment again and brought you some more clothes and a chocolate bar," Alex said as she handed Zoey a big tote bag.

Zoey looked through it but didn't find the chocolate. "Where is it?"

Alex looked around the room before pulling the candy out of her bra.

"I didn't think they'd let you have it."

"You're hilarious," Zoey laughed as she opened the wrapper and took a bite.

Alex walked over to her nightstand and picked up the camera. "Where did you get this?"

"Oh, I guess people donated gifts and decorations for Christmas so that was my gift," Zoey shrugged. "It's a cheap instant camera. I don't know what I'm going to do with it here. It's not like there's anything to take photos of. Anyway, let me show you all my notes," she pulled took her notebook out of the nightstand drawer and gave it to Alex.

To Zoey's surprise, when Alex flipped through the pages, she was incredibly shocked at how much Zoey had actually remembered so far.

"You really have remembered a lot since last week... you know that, right? Look at all these pages you have filled up," Alex said as she flipped through them.

"But I need to remember EVERYTHING. I'm growing really impatient here... I'm not even a patient person to begin with," Zoey sighed. "I'm starting to feel like I actually do belong in this place."

Alex shook her head, "No... no, you definitely don't belong here. You're going to get out of here, sis."

"Dr. Hall said she can't let me leave until she believes I'm not a danger to anyone or myself... but I feel like I need to remember why I acted the way I did to make her realize that I'm not like that... I'm not a dangerous person! I can't believe I'm still here!" Zoey's eyes became watery, and they sat in silence as both the girls felt stumped on what to do. Alex could tell that Zoey was starting to lose faith so for the remainder of their time together, she tried to think of anything that could possibly help, and they went over her notes over and over again.

However, the hour passed quickly before Tee walked into her room and told Alex it was time to leave.

Zoey rolled her eyes and fell back on the floor.

"Ugh! Can I just leave with her this time, please?" she groaned.

"Sorry," Tee shrugged.

Alex stood up and looked down at Zoey.

"I'm sorry too," she sighed.

"Ah, it's not your fault. You go... I'll be here when you get back," Zoey spread her arms out dramatically, "lying on this floor, trapped in my thoughtless thoughts."

"Your thoughtless thoughts will turn back into thoughtful thoughts, I promise. We're going to get you out of here. Keep writing and thinking... call me tomorrow. Don't lose hope. Love you!" Alex reminded her as she went to follow Tee out of the room.

"Love you too," Zoey called out, still lying hopelessly on the floor.

CHAPTER 11

DEC 21st

7:15 A.M.

"Breakfast time, breakfast time! Wake up, everybody!" Kelsey sang out in the hallway. She was so loud that Zoey could hear her clearly through her closed door.

"Ugh, I hate my life now," Zoey whined as she rolled out of bed.

She went into the bathroom and tried to turn on the shower, but it still wasn't working. However instead of getting mad, she brushed out her hair, put it into a high bun, and then headed to the cafeteria, as she tried to remind herself to stay calm.

When she walked in, Destiny was already sitting at a table wearing a full face of makeup. She wore bright red eyeshadow, dark red lipstick, and gold highlighted cheeks. Zoey got her food and then sat down across from her.

"Here comes the cat lady," Destiny whispered as the nurse approached their table.

"I heard that Destiny. I am not a cat lady," the nurse said.

Then she looked at Zoey and held the pill out towards her.

Zoey rolled her eyes and opened her palm.

"I know the routine," she sighed and dropped the pill in her mouth.

"Have a lovely breakfast," the nurse said.

She turned away and Destiny laughed extra loud, purposely to annoy her.

As Zoey took a bite of her food, she spotted a new patient in the cafeteria.

"Hey, who is that? I don't think I've seen him yet."

There was an extremely skinny young man in a hospital gown standing up next to the table behind them. He had a bald head and looked to be in his early twenties.

Destiny turned around and gasped. "OH NO!"

She whipped her head back towards Zoey and widened her eyes. "That spawn of the devil is back! THAT'S JOHNATHON! We have to be careful around him!"

"Who-- who's Johnathon?" Zoey questioned.

"Oh, the tale of Johnathon," Destiny sang out in a whisper, "he gets committed every few weeks, but the last time he was here," she shook her head, "oh girl, he is crazy with a capital C! Emphasis on the cray part! Look at him! He NEVER stops walking!"

They both looked at Johnathon who was now pacing back and forth in a small circle.

"I can see that..." Zoey observed.

"Yeah, he's a freak. Stay away from him. He gets these spasm attacks, kind of like Derek but like ten times worse... See! He's doing it right now! It looks like he's having a seizure! He's going to start crying in three, two, one-"

"Ah!" Johnathon busted out into tears and his body began twitching just as Destiny predicted.

The cafeteria nurse jumped up from her seat and hurried over to his side.

"Johnathon, it's okay. Relax. You just need to sit down! Sit down Johnathon!" she told him, but he picked up the pace, enlarging his circle.

"Yeah, cafeteria now," she said into her radio then turned her attention back to him. "Johnathon sit down, right now!"

"NOOO! I can't sit! I can't!" he said as his walk turned into a jog.

Destiny and Zoey exchanged wide glances and slowly slid down the bench further away from him.

Why the hell am I still here with these people?

"Do you want a shot, Johnathon?" The nurse raised her voice just as Tee and another guard came rushing into the room.

"NO! I don't want a shot!"

Johnathon turned to run but the second guard grabbed him by the arms. Tee held his legs down and turned him over to his stomach on the floor.

The nurse quickly bent down and stuck the same horse-like tranquilizer needle that they used on Derek, into Johnathon's back and his screams fell silent while his body stopped twitching. Tee picked him up and threw him over his shoulder, then carried him out of the cafeteria.

"See what I mean?" Destiny shook her head.

"Oh yeah… I do, I see what you mean…" Zoey stared at the doorway in shock.

2:15 P.M.

Tina and Lisa danced around the activity room while they sang into the set of fake microphones that Tina received as a present from the donations box.

"Join us, Zoey!" Lisa called out as soon as she walked through the door.

But before Zoey could answer, Debra cut off the music.

"Would you prefer to listen to music inside or go OUTSIDE and listen to music?" Dr. Hall asked everyone as she stood in the doorway.

"Outside! Outside!" many patients called out.

"Outsides for idiots!" Miriam scoffed as she turned the TV up louder.

"That's okay, Miriam. You can stay inside. Your choice," Dr. Hall said, "but to those of you who do want to go outside, the weather's very nice today so let's go!"

Everyone except for Will and Miriam went to follow Dr. Hall out of the room.

"I think those two belong together. I don't think you're right for him," Zoey said to Destiny, who was glaring right at them.

"I think you're right, Zo Zo! Let's go have fun," she said as she put her arm around Zoey's shoulders and looked back towards the couch, "WITHOUT THEM!"

They followed everyone out to the courtyard and as soon as they stepped outside, Dr. Hall told everyone to sit down for group circle.

"Why can't we just enjoy being outside without any stupid emotion talk?" Tina argued.

"Because we haven't had one in a few days and I thought it would be nice to switch it up and talk outside for once," Dr. Hall said. "Today, I'd like to talk about our past. Let's talk about why you're all sitting here right now."

Tina pointed to her sister. "We're sitting here because the system is a piece of crap!"

"I second that!" Destiny added, "you think living with random people is a good idea? My foster mom literally came from the devil himself! She drove me insane."

"That's why you tried to jump out of the car, right?" Kelsey laughed.

"Kelsey, until you're ready to be as pretty as me, don't talk to me," Destiny snapped.

"Tina was talking first, let her continue," Dr. Hall interrupted the girls.

"What I was going to say was, my sister and I wouldn't be in here if the judges would have just let us live by ourselves. We practically did so our whole lives anyway!" Tina pouted.

"That's why we started the fire," Lisa whispered.

"Shh!" Tina hissed.

"Okay, thank you for sharing ladies," Dr. Hall said. "Why don't you go now, Kelsey?"

Kelsey sat up and pushed her greasy hair out of her face. "My past is nothing like all of yours. When I met Jeremy, everything changed.

He changed my life forever. He's been with me for years now, but my sister doesn't believe me."

"That's because Jeremy's a ghost," Destiny blurted out.

Dr. Hall gave her a warning look and Destiny covered her mouth.

"YES! Jeremy is a ghost, but he's MY GHOST!" Kelsey said loudly.

She looked over to her left, mumbled something, and then nodded.

"He doesn't like you Destiny."

Destiny rolled her eyes and laughed dramatically.

"Okay, Zoey would you like to go next?" Dr. Hall asked.

I'd like to get the hell out of here.

Zoey sighed. "Uh, I somehow lost my memory of a day and here I am."

"How do you forget just one day?" Kelsey asked.

That's the magical question.

"Now you didn't forget the whole day, Zoey," Dr. Hall interrupted, "you were just telling me about some dreams that help you recall what you did right?"

Zoey rubbed her eyes, "ugh, yes kind of. But I still don't remember everything."

"I'm helping her with that!" Destiny volunteered.

Shut up before Dr. Hall classifies me on your level of crazy.

"That's fantastic girls!" Dr. Hall smiled.

"It's going to rain again soon! Can we please enjoy outside a little bit more before it starts to thunder?" Destiny asked as the clouds were starting to roll in and the sky was turning gloomy.

Dr. Hall smiled. "Destiny's right. Go have fun."

"Thank you, Dr. Hall!" Lisa exclaimed.

She leaped up from the grass along with everyone else who dispersed from the group.

Zoey went over to the bench with her camera and sat down to watch everybody. Johnathon was pacing back and forth in big steps. Lisa and Tina were playing a card game in the grass and there were three other female patients stretched out into yoga poses by the garden.

"Debra, can you play some more Christmas music? I need to practice my big number!" Destiny asked as she stood on her toes in a ballet stance against the fence.

Debra happily agreed and turned up the portable speakers that she brought outside from the activity room.

As soon as the music sounded, Destiny broke out into a series of leg kicks and spins in a very unchoreographed manner. Zoey snapped a quick photo of her, then looked over at Lisa and Tina and took a photo of them. Just as she was about to take one of Johnathon, the sound of thunder suddenly shook the sky and nearly everyone except Zoey screamed.

"Okay, let's go, everyone. I'm sorry but it's time to go back in!" Debra called out after she turned off the music.

Destiny kicked at the fence. "Are you kidding me?! Just when I was getting my spin correct!"

At least I had a few minutes of fresh air...

Zoey was tired of feeling emotional, tired of crying for no reason, and of walking the same halls repeatedly. So, to stay out of her thoughts, she decided to follow Destiny around.

"So, what's this big number you have planned for Christmas?" she asked as she watched Destiny dance light on her feet down the hall.

"Oh, I plan to wow everyone with a special dance on Christmas day! I need to get it exactly right! How am I looking?"

Like you have no idea what you're doing.

"Like you have A LOT of energy, Destiny," Zoey smiled.

"Thanks!" Destiny jumped with joy.

I did not mean it as a compliment.

"YES! Derek's door is closed! Let's mess with him," she giggled.

"And how are we going to do that?"

"Shh," Destiny whispered.

She hunched down low and tip-toed over to Derek's door. Then she looked over at Zoey and let out a slight giggle before knocking rapidly on his door.

"Run, run, run!" she whispered as she ran back towards Zoey.

She grabbed her by the arm and spun her around, then dragged her back down the hallway and ducked behind the corner. They watched Derek poke his head out of his door and then slowly step into the hall.

"Hey! Who just knocked? We were busy here!" he yelled out.

"Derek, NO yelling," a nurse scolded as she walked by.

"He HATES when people knock," Destiny chuckled. She slowly peeked around the corner. "Okay, we're clear. He went back to his room."

First, I was playing dress-up, now I'm playing ding-dong ditch… what has my life become?

6:00 P.M.

"You need to eat. Stop feeding them! They don't even need food," Tina said to Lisa, who held a forkful of chicken up to one of her doll's mouths.

"NO!" Lisa pouted, now holding both dolls tightly to her chest. "They need food just like you and me. I ate enough already. Stop being a big sister!"

"Ladies!" Destiny called out from the doorway as she stood in a superwoman pose.

"Oh my…" Zoey dropped her fork as soon as she spotted her.

Destiny's cheeks were covered in red blush, accompanied by bright red lips and gold eyeshadow. Her hair was pulled back into a high bun and she was wearing a velvet green tracksuit, the kind that grew popular back in the late 1990's / early 2000's.

"I didn't even know those things still existed," Zoey thought aloud as she stared at her clothes.

"Like my look?" Destiny twirled around. "Will's going to really notice me now. That's for sure!" she said as she spotted Will, sitting at another table. "I'll be back!"

Tina sighed, "you know what, I'm tired. I'm going back to my room. Lisa, finish eating, then go to bed!"

"Don't tell me what to do!" Lisa pouted.

Tina suddenly threw her plate to the floor in aggravation. "I'll tell you whatever I want to tell you, sister!"

"Hey! Girls do NOT start right now," the cafeteria nurse warned from her corner.

"UGH! I HATE THIS PLACE!" Tina marched out of the cafeteria.

Lisa, who was now in tears, crawled under the lunch table in a fetal position with her dolls.

Okay and that's my cue to leave.

Zoey slowly got up from the table with her tray, threw out the rest of her food, then went back to her room.

12:15 A.M.

Between the nurses' footsteps in the hall, random outbursts from other patients, and Zoey's thoughts, it was nearly impossible to sleep. After what seemed like hours of tossing and turning, she looked at the clock on the wall and instantly got aggravated when she saw that it was only a quarter past midnight.

Maybe someone fixed my shower...

She got out of bed and went to the bathroom. She turned on the shower and was well surprised when relatively warm water started pouring out. So, she closed her bathroom door, undressed, and jumped in.

"Oh wow, I look like an ape," she said to herself as she noticed the visible hairs on her legs and underarms.

I never wished to have a razor so badly before.

Just a few minutes into her shower, Zoey thought she heard a door opening so she poked her head out from behind the curtain. Her bathroom door was closed but now she felt paranoid, so she quickly rinsed off.

Just as she was turning off the water, this time, she heard footsteps outside of the bathroom door.

"Who's there?" She poked her head out again and saw the doorknob starting to turn.

"HEY! I'm in the shower! Get out!" she yelled just as a nurse opened the door.

"Showering isn't allowed at this time. Shower cut off is at 9:00 p.m.," she said.

"Okay, I'll get out in a minute," Zoey said, hastily.

"No, you'll get out now," the nurse insisted.

"Okay, then can you please leave so I can actually get out? I am naked, ya know!"

"I'll be waiting outside," the nurse said.

"I'm sure you will," Zoey muttered.

No privacy around here.

She stepped out of the shower, quickly changed into a pair of leggings and a sweatshirt, then walked out to find the nurse sitting on her bed.

No boundaries either.

The nurse got up, smiled, and walked out of the room without closing the door.

Out of anger, Zoey stomped over to the door and closed it with so much force that the sound of its slam made the nurse come back right away.

"Do you have a problem, young lady?" the nurse demanded after swinging the door back open.

Zoey crossed her arms. "I have problems with people who barge into bathrooms without knocking."

"Then, you can keep your door open for the rest of the night," the nurse said, then walked away.

Zoey half-heartedly wanted to slam the door again, but she told herself to be the bigger person and instead, went to lay in bed.

It's just one night. I probably wasn't going to sleep anyways.

CHAPTER 12

DEC 22nd

7:00 A.M.

After sleeping for only four hours, Kelsey's singing jolted Zoey awake and she instantly realized that her door was open. She hurriedly jumped out of bed and ran to close her door but was too late as Kelsey already spotted it open as she was passing by. She skipped backward and stopped in front of Zoey.

"It's breakfast time," Kelsey insisted, bobbing her head up and down.

"Yes, I know that. I think the whole world knows that, Kelsey. Thank you for alerting all of us," Zoey sighed.

She went to close the door, but Kelsey put her foot in front of it.

"I'll see you in the cafeteria," Kelsey stepped closer to her. "ZOEY."

Then she continued on her way.

Deep breaths... just get through today without killing that woman.

Zoey tied her hair into a high bun, then grabbed her camera from the nightstand before going to get her breakfast.

"Maybe you'll help distract me," she said as she held the camera in her hand, "and now I'm talking to inanimate objects... Guess I do belong here."

She left the room and headed towards the cafeteria.

Just as she was on her way, Will stepped out of his room.

"Tell Destiny to leave me alone," he demanded.

"Uh, not my problem, sorry," Zoey said and kept walking.

"No, seriously. I want to be left alone. Tell her for me," he insisted.

She stopped walking. "Uh, no. You tell her yourself."

"I'm serious," he said with a sinister look. "Tell her I'm NOT interested."

He walked into the cafeteria clenching his fists.

Maybe I SHOULD tell Destiny to stay away from him...

"BREAAAAKFAAAST TIMMMME!" Kelsey sang out, louder from down the other hall.

I can't deal with these people anymore...

Zoey turned around to go back towards her room but bumped right into Destiny.

"Ow girl! Watch out! You almost knocked me down, Zo Zo," she gasped.

"Uh, sorry Destiny. I was heading back to my room," Zoey said, irritably.

Her stomach rumbled loudly, and Destiny gave her a suspicious look.

"You sure you don't want food instead?" she asked, pouting her lips.

I am REALLY hungry... If I skip breakfast, being hungry will only end up making me more agitated...

"I guess you're right," Zoey sighed. "Let's go get breakfast."

"Yay, let's go!" Destiny clapped. She skipped towards the cafeteria, dragging Zoey along with her.

They walked in and went in to stand in line behind Will, who stood firmly with his hands in his jean pockets, staring straight ahead. Destiny hit Zoey's arm repeatedly and giggled like a high school girl. Will, who obviously could hear her, turned just his head enough to see behind him.

"Leave me alone," he scoffed.

Destiny stopped giggling, placed both hands on her hips, and straightened her torso.

"*I AM* leaving you alone. I didn't even touch you."

"Just leave me alone. I'm not interested," Will said, clearly very aggravated.

Destiny stepped in front of him. "Listen, WILL! I AM NOT interested in you either!"

Maybe they do belong together...

"Whatever," he mumbled and brushed by her with his food.

"I'm not hungry anymore," Destiny pouted as tears started to fall from her face.

She covered them with her hands and stormed out of the cafeteria.

I can't believe I'm still in this place...

Zoey stepped forward, received a plate of food, then went over to sit with Lisa and Tina.

"My babies were haaaangry!" Lisa exclaimed as she pretended to feed them.

"No, they weren't," Tina rolled her eyes.

"OOOOH! Have you taken any pictures with this yet?" Lisa asked while grabbing Zoey's camera off the table.

Zoey grabbed it back out of her hand. "No, not really. I don't even know why I brought it..." she said as she held the camera in her hands and admired the room.

Will was sitting at a table alone. Kelsey sat at another table with two other patients. Miriam's food fell out of her mouth as she mumbled to herself. Derek and Johnathon paced back and forth together. They must have passed each other least six times before the cafeteria nurse told them to stop and eat their food. Amazingly enough, they both listened.

"You know what? I think I will take a photo," Zoey said.

She walked over to the door and held the camera up to her eye. She snapped a photo, then returned to the table as she waited for it to develop.

"Those instant cameras are so cool!" Lisa said, fascinated as she watched the photo pop out of the top of the camera. "Oh! can I see the picture, PLEASE?!" she begged.

Instead of answering her, Zoey watched the image develop, then looked around at everyone in the room again, then back at the photo.

"Never would I ever thought this would happen to me," she murmured.

"Soooo, can I see it or not?" Lisa asked, impatiently.

"Patience sister, Zoey's having a moment," Tina said.

Zoey's thoughts broke at the sound of her name and she gave the photo to Lisa.

"Hey! That's us, Tina! Look!" She shoved it in front of her sister's face.

Tina pushed it away. "I see it."

Zoey finished up her food a few minutes later, said goodbye to the girl's and then went to walk out of the cafeteria. Just as she reached the door, the nurse stopped her for her medication and dropped it in her mouth, then walked out of the room, immediately hiding it in her waistband.

Just as she did so, Kelsey came out of the cafeteria behind her. "Hey! I saw you!"

Not this girl again…

Zoey turned around, arms crossed. "And what exactly did you see, Kelsey?"

Kelsey stepped closer to her. "I saw you," she poked her chest, "hide that pill in your waistband."

"You saw nothing, psycho."

She removed Kelsey's finger and turned to walk back towards her room, but Kelsey grabbed her shoulder.

"Are you kidding me?" The feeling of Kelsey's hand on Zoey's body instantly aggravated her.

"DO. NOT. MESS. WITH. ME," she warned.

I can't punch her… I'll never get out of here if I do.

Kelsey stepped back in one swift motion. "Carry on to your room then."

Zoey marched by without saying anything.

I have to get out of here before I kill that woman.

2:00 P.M.

Zoey sat next to Will and Miriam as they watched a cartoon talking fox and sloth run around on TV. Every few minutes, Miriam would turn up the volume until it reached a loudness that Debra didn't like and when Debra would ask her to turn it down, Miriam would softly laugh, then slowly lower the volume. Zoey seemed to be the only one to notice that she was doing it clearly out of spite.

Suddenly, Kelsey threw a puzzle piece to the floor and started banging on the table with both hands.

"It's not working! Pieces are missing! Help me find them!" she cried out and leaped up from her seat.

Debra walked over towards her very calmly. "Kelsey, honey sit back down. Please calm down, I'll help you find them."

Kelsey sat back down but continued to slam her palms against the table.

"You need to find them right now!" Now!" she demanded.

"Please do not bang on the table. That is not your property," Debra scolded.

"I NEED TO FIND THE PIECES! I NEED TO COMPLETE THE PUZZLE!"

I need you to find her now…

Zoey sat almost paralyzed on the couch as she watched Kelsey act in such an irrational fashion. Watching her hit the table and demand for the puzzle pieces suddenly prompted Zoey's memory of the police station.

I was demanding and yelling at the cops... just like Kelsey is right now...

Kelsey grew more impatient. Her feet tapped against the floor, and she slammed her fists repeatedly, on the table.

She abruptly stood up and tried to flip the table over, but she failed as it was bolted to the floor, which made her angrier. "AHHHHH!!!!" she screamed and began smacking her face with both hands... and as Zoey watched, she started to remember acting the same way.

I slapped myself when I went for a walk in my dream... and I did that at the police station...

As Kelsey continued to smack herself, Zoey felt the hard sting on her face all over again.

"*You need to help me! I saw my mother downtown!*"

"*Is she missing?*"

"*No! She's alive! I found her!*"

"*What's your name miss?*"

"*Just go find her!*"

Zoey could remember the force against her fists, her cheeks stinging, the look of the police woman's face, the hands of a male officer, the cuffs against her wrists... and all at once, the full memory of being at the police station came back to her.

"*Do you have anyone to call Miss?*"

"*Call my mom! Go find her already! Do your damn jobs!*"

"*Go ahead and take her. I'll call psych.*"

"*Call my mom!*"

"Zoey, are you okay dear? What is the matter? Zoey?" Debra asked.

"She was hyperventilating just a minute ago. You missed it during all the Kelsey craziness, idiot," Miriam said.

Zoey could not feel her whole body shaking. She did not even hear Debra speaking. All she could do was stare at Kelsey as she remembered acting just like her.

"What are you looking at!?" Kelsey demanded.

"Zoey, honey, would you like to talk or take your anxiety medication right now?" Debra asked.

Zoey tried to speak but the words could not come out. All she could do was keep staring in Kelsey's direction.

"Tee, can you take her back to her room, please? I'll have a nurse bring in her medication. I think she should lay down," Debra said.

"Let's go," Tee gestured towards the door and Zoey slowly stood up, feeling like she was about to collapse.

She couldn't feel her legs, her arms, or even her face. Everything felt numb.

Tee helped her back to her room and when they walked in, a nurse was already there with her medication. Zoey took it without even thinking and crawled into her bed, emotionless. She closed her eyes and let the memory of hurting herself replay in her mind until the medicine kicked in and knocked her right out.

5:30 P.M.

Zoey woke up to the sound of someone knocking at her door.

"Hey, it's me girl!" Destiny called out.

"Come in," Zoey groaned. She pulled the covers over her head and turned to her side.

Destiny walked in and sat on the foot of the bed. "Zo Zo, I wanted to see if you were okay?"

"I'm good," she mumbled from underneath the blanket.

"Are you sure? You can talk to me, ya know. Did you remember something? It looked like you remembered something, or you saw a ghost," Destiny paused, "wait, you didn't see one, right?"

Zoey pulled the blanket off over her head.

"You're full of questions, Destiny."

A huge smile spread across Destiny's face.

"THANKS! Curiosity never killed the cat!"

I'll let her think that.

"Right… Well yeah, I did remember something. I remember being at the police station now…" Zoey sat up. "Ugh, what time is it? My heads killing me."

"It's 5:30," Destiny answered. "You've been knocked out since Tee took you out of the activity room. At least you got to miss group circle. Derek told us a story about one of the people inside of him."

I'm not sorry I missed that.

Zoey looked at the clock. "Wait, 5:30 already?! I'm missing my session."

She tried to get out of bed but felt a wave of dizziness, so she laid back down.

"At least you're not seeing ghosts," Destiny laughed.

Zoey pulled the cover back over her head. "I think I'd rather prefer seeing ghosts instead."

"Then you'd really be like Kelsey!" Destiny giggled.

"NO!" Zoey shot up from the bed, despite feeling dizzy. "I'm NOT like her. I can't be like her."

Destiny leaned in and hugged Zoey real tight. "It's okay Zo Zo. You're not like her. It's okay."

But I'm not okay… none of this is okay.

Zoey pulled away, wiped her eyes, and got out of bed.

"There's still time left. I'm going to go see Dr. Hall."

"Good luck!" Destiny cheered as Zoey stumbled out of her room and marched straight to Dr. Hall's office.

"It's Zoey! I was sleeping! Let me in," she called out frantically while knocking on her door.

Dr. Hall opened the door a few seconds later.

"Oh, come on in Zoey. I know you were sleeping. It's okay, no worries."

Zoey walked in and immediately started telling her about what happened in the activity room.

"I saw Kelsey acting so erratic and it made me remember that I acted the same way towards the cops," she said through sobs, "but I just-- I just don't see why I was so irrational, so-- so mad at them…"

Dr. Hall typed something for a minute then turned her attention back to Zoey and gave her one of those caring sincere looks that Zoey found annoying.

"Zoey, I think you had a momentary lapse of insanity," Dr. Hall said while she rested her hands on the desk.

Insanity? A lapse of insanity?

"Wh-- what do you mean?" Zoey stuttered.

"I believe that all the stress you've gone through... and not grieving your mother properly, have caught up to you all at once which caused a trigger to your brain," Dr. Hall paused, "It momentarily shut down."

"So, you're telling me that my brain just stopped working because I work too much, and I miss my mom?" Zoey asked in disbelief.

"To put it shortly, your brain needed a break," Dr. Hall nodded sincerely.

She was looking firmly in Zoey's eyes, which began to make Zoey uncomfortable.

"I-I, I don't get it," she stammered, feeling utterly confused and tired. "I've been way more stressed in my life before... I don't understand why this would happen now."

"Because it built up in you Zoey. You work alone... You live alone. You deal with all your stress on your own, and you don't seem to have a real coping mechanism for any of it," she continued. "I want you to really focus on quieting and controlling your mind for the next few days."

"FEW DAYS?" Zoey gasped.

"Yes, like I have been telling you. And then, we'll see how you progress," Dr. Hall answered.

Tears welled up in Zoey's eyes. "But I… I just want to go home."

"I need to make sure you're okay mentally before you go home, and I don't think you're quite there yet. The cops deemed you as violent to yourself and others but honestly Zoey, I do not see you that way. I don't believe you're violent. I believe you just need to gain control of your emotions and focus on yourself… then you will be stable enough to go back home. Everything will be okay."

But it's not okay…

The printer on Dr. Hall's desk spit out a piece of paper and she handed it to Zoey.

"Here is a list of ways to cope with stress and anxiety. I want you to read them and see if any of them might work for you," she said.

Zoey took the paper and examined it.

Take deep breaths. Count to one hundred. Count backward from one hundred. Exercise. Listen to music. Yoga. Meditate. Journal.

Zoey stuck the paper in her hoodie pocket. "I'm gonna go back to my room now," she muttered and walked out of the office, then ran back to her room.

As soon as she got there, she screamed into her pillow.

"AHHHH! "Why, life why!" she sobbed.

Tears streamed down her tingling face as she kicked and punched uncontrollably at the bed like a child.

"What am I doing? Why am I acting this way?"

She slammed the bed with both of her fists and her breathing became short.

A sudden feeling of nausea started to hit, and she stumbled over to the bathroom just in time to throw up in the toilet.

"Why is this happening to me?" she cried out as she flushed.

She sat back against the bathroom wall with her eyes closed. Between the realization of being stuck in the hospital to the sudden real memory of yelling at the cops, Zoey felt like she was on the verge of really losing her mind. The recollection of it all was beginning to overwhelm her.

"I'm losing control of myself..."

Zoey stood up and looked in the mirror which she was surprised to see a very unrecognizable image of herself. Her hair had fallen loose out of its high bun. Her normally pale skin was now even paler, and her left cheek was accompanied by two large pimples. There were dark bags under her eyes, as Destiny had pointed out the other day. Her eyes were bloodshot and glossy, and sweat and tears dripped off her chin.

Do I really belong here?

She stopped sniffling and blew her runny nose, washed her face, and then went to lay back down in bed.

As she laid there, her thoughts ran. Out of anger, she chucked the pillow across the room, and it hit the lamp on the nightstand which fell to the ground, startling her.

I need to control myself… I can't act like this.

She quickly got out of bed and went to pick up the lamp, thankful that it wasn't broken.

Just as she was crawling back under the covers, Tee opened her door.

"Why don't you ever knock?" Zoey groaned.

"I heard a loud noise. Are you okay? Did something fall?"

His eyes inspected the room.

Zoey pulled the covers over her body. "I'm fine. Nothing fell," she muttered.

"I see your pillow on the ground," Tee remarked.

"That is correct, you are very observant," Zoey sighed.

"Let me know if you need anything," he said as he went to close the door.

Zoey sat up. "Wait actually, yes I do need something," she said. "My head is killing me. Can I get something for it?"

"I'll have a nurse come by," he said and walked out of the room.

Five minutes later, a nurse walked into her room with a small pill and a water bottle.

Zoey skeptically examined it and made double sure that it was just a regular ibuprofen before swallowing.

She laid in bed for the rest of the night trapped in her thoughts, scared to remember what else she was forgetting.

CHAPTER 13

DEC 23rd

7:10 A.M.

Zoey woke up a few minutes past seven and was surprised that she hadn't heard Kelsey singing yet. She got out of bed, took a quick shower, changed into leggings, and a new hoodie from the bag of clothes that Alex brought, then grabbed her notebook and camera and headed to the cafeteria.

Just as she was walking out of her door, Tee came running past her. Zoey looked towards the direction he ran and saw a nurse and another guard rushing over from the other end of the hall, near Derek's room. They all met in the middle and stopped in front of Johnathon, who was running in place, slapping his knees with more force every time they went up in the air.

"My feet hurt," he kept repeating.

Tee and the other guard grabbed Johnathon by his arms. He started to kick away and almost hit the nurse in front of him, so Tee let go and went to grab his feet. As Tee reached for them, Johnathon kicked again and this time, was just an inch away from missing Tee's chest before he got hold of his legs. He pinned Johnathon down to the floor while the other guard firmly held his arms down and the nurse, who had been ready with that large needle, promptly stabbed Johnathon in his right arm. He cried out for a moment then fell asleep and Tee released his grip, leaving the other guard to carry Johnathon back to his room.

Amid it all, Zoey had taken a photo of the whole scene. As she waited for it to develop, she continued down the hallway. Johnathon's door was open when she walked by and she could see him lying on his stomach with his mouth wide open, sound asleep.

"They came to get him... they're coming to get us too," whispered Derek from the doorway of his room.

Zoey stepped closer to him and stared sinisterly. "They already came for me," she whispered back.

Derek gasped and ducked back into his room, closing the door behind him.

That was satisfying.

Zoey looked down at the photo, which was now fully developed and busted out into a loud laugh when she saw the image of Tee. His eyes were wide, and his head was pulled back as Johnathon's feet were in the air.

She walked into the cafeteria and went to stand in line behind Miriam.

"This food is nasty! Always the same thing... we're not animals ya know!" she complained.

The lady behind the food line glared back at her, then slapped two scrambled eggs and a piece of toast on her plate without saying a word.

"Ugh, idiots!" Miriam tossed the tray to the ground and stormed out of the line.

"Miriam, get back over there and pick that up!" the cafeteria nurse called out.

"BITE ME!" Miriam scoffed, then marched out of the cafeteria.

Zoey covered her mouth as she tried not to burst out laughing.

I think I'm starting to like Miriam.

Zoey stepped forward and got her plate of eggs and hash browns, then carefully stepped over the food that was left on the floor from Miriam and then went to sit next to Destiny.

"Are you okay, Destiny?" she asked as she sat down across from her.

"No, Zo Zo. I am not okay," Destiny said, dramatically. She closed her eyes, inhaled deeply, held it for a moment, and then exhaled.

"I think Will doesn't like me."

You're just realizing that?

"Oh, well I don't think it's you Destiny... I think he just," Zoey paused, "has a certain type and... you're not it?"

"That's a load of crap. I'm beautiful," she pouted.

"That is true Destiny. You are... but I think maybe Will might be, um..." Zoey lowered her voice to a whisper, "gay."

Destiny's mouth fell open and her eyes grew wide.

"No way!" she whispered back. "Why do you say that?"

To make you feel better.

"Just a hunch," Zoey shrugged.

Destiny flipped her hair. "Well, then. I guess I don't feel so bad after all."

"Here, I have something to show you," Zoey said. She took the photo of Johnathon out of her pocket. "I took this on the way here. I think it will make you smile."

Destiny looked at the photo and busted out laughing just like Zoey had when she first saw it. "I-- I can't believe you-- you," Destiny said in between laughs, "got that shot. It's so perfect!"

Tears fell from her eyes, she thought it was so funny.

Zoey looked at the photo again and realized she was right. For a little instant camera, she was surprised at the shots she was getting. But then again, she had not touched a digital camera in over a week, so maybe that's why she felt that way. Whatever the reason was, she did not mind. Taking photos started to make her feel better. Just holding something familiar that she was used to in her daily life lifted her mood. Thinking about photography made Zoey think about her clients who were not going to receive their photos by Christmas, which was just two days away.

"Well, at least I warned them. There goes all my money," she winced.

"You talk to yourself a lot," Destiny remarked.

Zoey rolled her eyes. "Yeah, I'm aware."

Just as Zoey began to eat her food, Kelsey came skipping into the cafeteria, making sure to give the girls a hard stare as she passed their table.

"There goes schizola," Destiny giggled.

The cafeteria nurse walked up to Kelsey with a pill bottle and Kelsey willingly opened her hand. The nurse dropped a pill into it and Kelsey took it right away, lifting her tongue right after to show the nurse that she swallowed.

"Here she comes noooow," Destiny said in a sing-song tone as the nurse began to approach her and Zoey.

The nurse handed Zoey and Destiny their medications and as soon as she turned away, Zoey immediately spit out the pill, then shoved it inside of her waistband.

"BUSTED!!!" Kelsey shouted.

Zoey turned around and saw that Kelsey was pointing directly at her.

Great, here we go again.

Kelsey skipped over happily, while the food on her tray rocked back and forth.

"I got your back girl," Destiny winked. She straightened up as Kelsey approached. "What's your problem with my Zo Zo?"

Kelsey slammed her tray onto the table. "Ha, Zo Zo! What kind of name is that?" she laughed.

I can't let this girl be the reason why I never get out of here...

"Can you just leave me the hell alone?" Zoey groaned.

"No, actually I can't! I don't like liars and you're a liar!" Kelsey stepped closer to her.

"Ladies!" the cafeteria nurse warned from her corner chair.

"I'm not doing anything!" Zoey put her hands in the air. "Look at her! She's the one starting with me. She's practically in my face!"

Kelsey threw her hands up to her cheeks, in shock. "I'm not the one fake swallowing pills!"

I'm going to kill this girl...

The nurse sighed in clear irritation and got up from her chair.

"Hide it," Destiny mouthed silently to Zoey.

Zoey went to push the pill further down in her leggings but right as she did so, Kelsey turned around and caught her. "SEE! SEE! She's shoving it down her pants!"

Yeah, this girl is dead to me.

"Do I need to call Tee over here ladies?" the nurse asked as she walked over.

Kelsey, who was clearly satisfied with causing as much trouble already, gave a sneering look. "I don't. Zoey, what do you think?"

I think you better sleep with one eye open.

"Is what Kelsey said true?" the nurse asked. She raised her chin.

"No, it's not true," Zoey lied. She glared at Kelsey. "I don't know why she keeps trying to mess with me. I'm taking my medication."

"LIAR!" Kelsey exclaimed.

"Kelsey, go sit down. I got this. Thank you for your concern," the nurse told her.

Kelsey gave a huge smile, before grabbing her tray and then skipped away.

The nurse turned her attention back to Zoey. "You'll be under watch for now on."

"What- what does that mean, now?" Zoey asked.

"I'll have to watch you take your pill from now on," the nurse responded.

Kelsey's a dead woman.

"Fine," Zoey mumbled as she had no energy to keep arguing.

Kelsey's going to regret ever meeting me.

Zoey took a few more bites of her food and then headed back to her room, feeling more frustrated than ever.

While on her way, she stopped in front of the phone in the hallway. Her hands were shaking so much from anger, that it took a few extra seconds to dial Alex's number. She fidgeted impatiently as she waited. "Pick up, pick up, pick up…"

"Hello?" Alex sounded half asleep when she answered.

"I'm going to kill that Kelsey girl!" Zoey blurted out.

"Woah, wait, what?"

"That psycho that fought with me!" Zoey groaned. "She keeps causing problems. Now I'm under watch when it comes to my medication. I wasn't taking this crap in the first place and now I really have to take it, all thanks to her!"

A few seconds of silence passed before Zoey spoke again. "I'm sorry. I woke you, didn't I? Are you off today?"

"Yeah, but it's okay. My alarm was supposed to go off in a few minutes anyway. So… why is this girl messing with you?" Alex asked.

"Because she's a lunatic," Zoey paused, "just like Miriam said, they're all lunatics."

"Right… well, try not to let her get to you. You're smarter than her. Don't let her get in the way of you getting out of there," Alex told her.

"Which speaking of, did you remember anything new? What has the Doctor said?"

"Oh yeah, uh, that," Zoey hesitated, "so, I remember being inside of the police station now... but just not actually arriving there."

"Oh, that's good!" Alex cheered.

"Yeah..." Zoey dragged out her words, "but not really because I was kind of acting a little insane... like Dr. Hall told me I was..."

"What do you mean?" Alex asked.

"So, in the activity room, Kelsey was slamming the table and demanding the nurse to find some puzzle pieces or something and when I watched her, I just somehow suddenly remembered being at the station. I was acting the same way... When I saw her freaking out, I literally felt numb... I just can't understand why I thought I saw my mom. That's the big mystery... I just don't get it. I was acting so irrational; you would not have even recognized me. I can barely recognize myself when I think about it... but it happened. I remember yelling at the cop..." she sighed. "It's weird to explain."

"You'll be okay, sis... I know it. At least you are remembering things," Alex tried to remind her.

Zoey's eyes became teary. "I was screaming at the cops... I was hyperventilating, crying... I just-"

"I really wish I could help you more," Alex interrupted. She sounded almost as defeated as Zoey. "I really wish I was with you that day or at least have spoken to you."

"Honestly, the photo you brought helped a lot, so you have helped... but anyway, I'm going to go," Zoey sniffled. "I need to figure out how to get out of here… like today. I can't do this anymore."

"I'll come by tonight, try not to hurt Kelsey in the meantime," Alex said.

"I'll do my best," Zoey hung up, then went back to her room.

When she got there, she placed her camera and the photo of Johnathon on her nightstand next to the other photos she had taken. Then she went into the bathroom and shimmied the small pill out of her pants to drop it into the toilet. She watched it twirl down as she flushed and shook her head.

"This is my life now," she sighed and looked over at herself in the mirror.

Even though she could now recall acting out at the station, it was just too hard to face. The fact that Zoey had acted in such a horrific way not only scared her… but nearly set her into shock. Her chest started feeling heavy and tears rolled down her cheeks. She inhaled deeply and counted out loud.

"One," then exhaled, "two," inhaled, "three," then exhaled. She looked up to the ceiling.

"Mom, if you're listening… I need you more than ever right now… I think I've actually gone crazy… I think I do belong here."

She wiped her teary eyes, livid at herself for being so emotional.

How could I let this happen to me?

Out of frustration, she smacked the wall with her right hand. It was a lot harder than she intended, which aggravated her even more. A full feeling of anxiousness began to take over, causing her body to tremble. She held her hand over her rapidly racing heart and walked out of the bathroom, now hyperventilating.

What is going on with me?

She dropped to her knees on the floor and began banging both her fists on the carpet like a child. Her hysterical cries became louder and the tears wouldn't stop flowing. She felt so disoriented that she had not even realized that she kept hitting the carpeted floor until a moment later when she noticed that her hands were nearly bleeding.

I hate my life right now… I hate the way I'm feeling…

She grabbed the empty water bottle from the night before, off the nightstand and threw it aggressively at the door just before Tee suddenly swung the door open.

"Do you need your medication?" he asked.

Zoey looked over at him and shook her head, no.

Tee picked up the water bottle off the floor. "Did you throw this?"

She shook her head again and wiped the tears from her cheeks.

"What happened to your hands?" he asked.

Zoey looked at her now bleeding hands and shook her head, disappointed in herself.

"Uh, nothing…" she quickly said as she hid them behind her back.

Tee knelt in front of her and held his hand out. "Come on, let me see."

Why did I do this to myself?

She slowly showed him her scratched up hands, which were still shaking.

"I'll be back to bandage you up," he said, then walked out of the room.

Zoey looked down at her sore hands which made her think about getting handcuffed in the station.

I'm doing it again... I did this at the station. Why can't I control myself?

She sat there lost in her thoughts until Tee came back with a first aid kit.

"Did punching the floor make you feel better?" he questioned.

"How do you know I punched the floor?" she asked through sniffles.

"Lucky guess," he shrugged as he poured rubbing alcohol on it.

The sting made her wince.

"Shouldn't a nurse be doing this?" she asked.

"Short staff today. Everyone else is busy," he said as he put a bandage on one hand.

Just my luck.

"You're back on open door order again," he said as he finished bandaging the other hand.

"Are you serious?" Zoey groaned, "why?!"

Tee looked down at her hand then back at her without saying a word.

"Fine." She rolled her eyes. "For how long?"

"You can discuss that with Dr. Hall later today," he said and packed his kit up. "Need anything before I leave?"

"I need more clean towels. I'm on my last one."

"I'll have someone bring them in later," he told her, then walked out of the room.

Zoey examined her hands, stunned at her actions.

I really just did this to myself...

Her body was shaking a lot less, but she still felt lightheaded and her face and body still slightly tingled.

I'm not in control of anything here... I can't eat when I want, shower when I want, I can't lock my door, I can't even in control of my emotions...

She closed her eyes and practiced the breathing exercises.

After a few deep breaths, Zoey stood up and went to wash her face in the bathroom. She fixed her hair into a high ponytail as she looked at her reflection through the mirror.

If I'm going to be crazy, I might as well entertain it.

She left the bathroom, grabbed her camera, and put a new set of film inside.

Let's see what insanity we can capture today...

Right when she walked into the hallway, she spotted Derek poking his head out of the doorway of his room. He was looking the opposite way, so she raised the camera to her eye.

"HEY! DEREK!" she yelled.

He whipped his head around frantically and Zoey took the photo right on time.

"SHE TOOK A PICTURE OF US!" he gasped, then slammed the door shut.

Zoey chuckled to herself as she watched the photo develop.

I'm never going to forget Derek… that is if I even get out of here...

Zoey continued her way down the hall. She turned the corner towards Destiny's room.

The door was open, but Destiny wasn't inside. So, Zoey left and went to walk down the second hallway. There were several patients with their doors open, including Miriam, who was sitting in a chair in front of her nightstand. She was shaking her head angrily and mumbling to herself. There was a man that looked to be in his early thirties, sitting cross-legged on the floor in the room next to hers, humming with his eyes closed. He wore his hospital gown backward; it tied around his neck and waist in the front, exposing his chest hair. Zoey snapped a photo of him, removed it from her camera and stuck it in her sweatshirt pocket. A few doors down, Lisa and Tina sat on the floor playing with their deck of cards.

"Hey, Zoey!" Lisa called out.

Zoey raised her camera and took a photo.

"OH! Did you just take a pic of us?" Lisa asked, excitedly.

"I did indeed Lisa, but you can't see it until Christmas. Sorry," Zoey shrugged.

If I'm stuck in here, I might as well have fun with it.

Lisa fake cried, "fiiiiine."

"What are you doing?" Tina gave Zoey an odd look.

"I'm not really sure... I'm just, I'm just on an adventure," Zoey answered as she held her arms out wide and backed away from the girls.

She turned around and took a left, back towards Destiny's room, not sure of what she was going to do next or where she was going.

Just as she was passing her door, Destiny popped up behind her.

"ZO ZO! Whatcha doin' over here?"

Zoey nearly leaped in the air when she heard Destiny speak.

Why am I not used to this by now?

"I'm just roaming around... I came to see what you were doing earlier but you weren't in your room," she sighed.

"I was in session..." Destiny answered. She looked at Zoey's hands. "Oh, my Zo Zo! What happened to your hands?" she gasped.

"Oh nothing, I just kind of lost it... I guess you could say I had a mental breakdown. Anyway, I'm bored," Zoey changed the subject and Destiny didn't seem to mind.

"OOOH! Let's do makeovers. We can take pictures!"

She clapped excitedly and skipped back into her room.

I should have known that was coming.

Trying to accept her new life in these small hallways, Zoey forced a smile and followed Destiny back to her room.

1:30 P.M.

It was a beautiful Florida day as Zoey stared out of the window at the courtyard. There was not a cloud in the sky and the sun beamed down, brightly. She watched a flock of birds flying through the courtyard and wished that she were one of them.

"Are we going outside today?" she asked Debra, who was sitting with another patient.

"Possibly. We'll see Zoey," Debra smiled.

"Then can I use the computer?" she asked.

Debra looked at the clock and made a contemplating face. "I guess…" she hesitated, "you're really not supposed to use the computers until activity time, but I'll make an exception."

She stood up and walked over to the computer.

"You only have a few minutes, so someone else can use it when they come in."

Zoey followed her over, sat down, and logged right into her email. There were a few unread ones from people who were inquiring about her photography services and one from Mrs. Vanetti. It read:

Zoey, I never received an email back from you. Is it possible that you have an assistant? Christmas is soon and I have not received your refund. I can't hire a new photographer now as it is too late. Please let me know when you can give me an update.

You did not receive an email back because I told you I was in the hospital and didn't have access to anything. You haven't received a refund because of that same reason idiot!

Zoey slammed the mouse against the mousepad out of anger.

"Zoey, please be careful with that. It's not yours," Debra warned in her innocent tone.

"Yes! I know this crap's not mine, DEBRA," Zoey snapped in a moment of frustration.

Debra looked at her stunned, like a deer in the headlights.

"Ugh, sorry Debra," Zoey exhaled.

"I think you should get off the computer now. Time's up, Zoey."

"No, no, no, no, please just another minute. Sorry, I'm fine. I just got upset for a second," Zoey sighed. "I didn't mean to snap on you."

Debra nodded, "okay, just a few more minutes, Zoey."

Zoey clicked away from her email and logged into her social media, which showed twice as many notifications as before. Many of them were from people that were concerned, and others were still calling her insane. She continued scrolling through her newsfeed until the video of herself popped up, which made her remember that one of her clients said they saw it. Instantly, her heart began racing and her breath became short.

I can't believe this is happening…

"Not again… not again," Zoey mumbled.

She placed a hand over her chest as she felt a panic attack coming on.

I'm okay. I can do this… breathe, breathe…

"It's okay Zoey, deep breaths," Debra said as she inhaled deeply. "Do it with me."

Zoey did as Debra said and they both inhaled and exhaled six times before she calmed down.

I'm such an idiot. Why is this happening to me?

"Sorry, I just - I," Zoey stammered.

Debra held a hand up. "No need for apologies. It happens."

I wish it didn't.

Zoey logged off her accounts, got up from her chair and then sat on the couch. A few moments later, the rest of the patients started to stroll in the room. Johnathon came charging in at a high-speed walk and continued to pace back and forth from one side of the room to the other.

"Jonathan, I think you should slow down," Debra said to him as he walked by her.

"I think you're right," he said in a deep breathless tone as he slowed down but still, kept pacing.

Tina, who looked visibly angry, walked in without Lisa for once. Destiny followed behind just a minute later and the girls both sat next to Zoey.

"Where's your other half, Tina?" Destiny asked.

Tina crossed her arms. "They gave her a shot. She's knocked out right now."

"Why this time?!" Destiny demanded.

This time?

"Because they're evil! She was just having a nightmare and they shot her up like she's an animal," Tina said while pointing to Tee, who had just walked into the room and was talking to Debra, "And he helped!"

He glanced over at the girls and continued speaking with Debra.

Tina's face was bright red and visibly full of rage.

"I'm freaking LIVID! I hate when they do that to her," she emphasized, "HATE IT!"

"That's their solution, to stab us when they can't handle us," Destiny said, shaking her head.

"I think I got the shot on my first night. That needle hurts," Zoey said as she thought about it. The memory was blurry, but the pain of the needle wasn't.

"Yeah, that crap is painful!" Tina whined.

"What's painful?" Kelsey asked, suddenly jumping into the conversation.

Destiny straightened up and pouted her lips. "None of your business!"

Kelsey rolled her eyes, then walked away.

"I'm really starting to hate that girl," Zoey said.

"I've hated her since day one!" Destiny leaped up from the couch with a sudden burst of energy.

"Oh, Debra! Can you please, please put some music on? I need to practice my dance!"

Debra turned on an old Christmas song and Destiny began to twirl around the room, arms spread in the air.

"Her dance moves suck," Miriam scoffed as she slumped down on the couch in place of where Destiny was sitting.

Jonathan, who was still pacing and looking at the ground while doing so, walked right into Destiny just as she came out of another twirl, and she dramatically fell to the floor.

"DEBRA! DID YOU SEE THAT?!" she gasped.

Oh, here we go...

"Jonathan honey, I think you should sit down now. Don't you?" Debra suggested.

He stopped pacing and looked over at Debra, then to Destiny who was still lying on the floor, whining in fake agony.

"I. think. I. do," he nodded.

Debra pulled out a chair next to her and he walked over to her quickly.

"Oh, and what about me?" Destiny stood up slowly. "I'm okay. Don't worry about me or anything!"

"You're fine Destiny," Debra smiled.

"Whatever, stupid Johnathon," Destiny muttered as she brushed nothing off her clothes. "Turn it up again, please."

Just as Debra was about to turn up the music, Dr. Hall walked in and announced that they could go outside for the remainder of activity time.

Most of the patients decided to stay in with Debra, except for Zoey and six others who followed Tee and another nurse into the courtyard.

When they got outside, Zoey leaned against the fence in the corner and watched everyone. Miriam sat on the bench, alone. Destiny continued to practice her dance, which looked different every time. Tina was punching the air, clearly still mad about Lisa being stuck inside, and two other patients, one being Miriam's meditating neighbor, sat alone in the grass on opposite sides of the courtyard.

Zoey took a picture of everyone and then put it in her sweatshirt pocket, wishing she had a shirt on under so she could take it off. Not even five minutes of being in the heat and she was already sweating. But although the sun was harsh, she inhaled the fresh air and sat down in the grass, not allowing the heat to annoy her. Instead, she was simply happy to be in the fresh air.

She closed her eyes and pictured walking outside in her neighborhood, while the morning sun shined bright. Coffee in hand, the palm trees blowing, the sun beaming, people around her.

I'm never taking the outside for granted ever again.

She opened her eyes and looked down at her bandaged hands.

The harsh reality of still being trapped in the hospital made her eyes fill with tears.

I can't let myself get out of control like that again…

4:40 P.M.

After being outside, Zoey went back to her room and took a shower. She brushed her wet hair out and dressed into a pair of leggings and a T-shirt, then went to Dr. Hall's office for her session.

"You're early today, Zoey. How are you doing?" Dr. Hall asked as she opened her office door.

"Uh yeah, I had nothing better to do," Zoey tried to force a smile. "Can I come in?"

"I see," Dr. Hall said as she gestured for her to walk in.

They both sat down on opposite sides of the desk.

"So, tell me about what happened to your hands," Dr. Hall said.

Zoey looked down at her bandages and exhaled.

"Well, I was doing yoga and when I stretched with my fists, they rubbed against the-" She looked up at Dr. Hall, who was looking at her quizzically.

Why am I even trying to lie? She obviously knows what I did. I can't do anything in private here...

"Fine. I hit the floor and scratched my hands," Zoey sighed. "They're fine though. I'm fine. It's just a few scratches."

Dr. Hall gave her a very sincere look. "Are you taking your medication?"

Of course, you would ask that.

"Ye-yeah," Zoey stammered.

"I have a report that said someone saw you hide your medication this morning?" Dr. Hall said.

"Someone? You mean Kelsey? She keeps messing with me for no reason. I never did anything to her," Zoey paused, "well besides fighting her... but she started that. I swear I'm taking my medicine."

"So, what led you to hurt yourself?" Dr. Hall asked as she began typing on her laptop.

"I really don't know. I just started getting uncontrollably ma-" Zoey stopped herself from saying the word *mad* at the thought of sounding too angry, "irritated about my situation... so I kind of uh, lost it for a moment... I guess."

Dr. Hall nodded, "why do you think it was so hard for you to control your aggravation?"

"I was irritated... not aggravated. I don't know... it just got really hard to control."

Zoey shifted in her chair.

"I don't understand why I'm feeling this way... It's becoming really hard to control my emotions... when I get irritated, I start crying... I've never acted this way before. I think it's because I'm stuck here. I don't belong here," Zoey sighed. "How much longer do I need to stay here until you'll allow me to go home?"

"We need to work on controlling your emotions and managing your stress in ways that are suitable for you at home before you can leave. Keep working on the anxiety relief techniques I gave you and we'll go from there," Dr. Hall said. She looked down at Zoey's hands. "The first step is learning not to hurt yourself when you're irritated... or hurting others."

Zoey slouched down in her chair as she felt speechless.

Dr. Hall smiled. "You got this, Zoey. I believe in you."

I'm glad someone does.

They ended the session shortly after and
Zoey left Dr. Hall's office, sobbing.

6:40 P.M.

As she sat down at a table alone with her
dinner, Zoey was glad to see that the cafeteria
was mostly deserted besides three other
patients. However, unfortunately, one of them
was Kelsey, who was intensely staring at her.

As soon as she began eating, the nurse
came over with her medication. Zoey grabbed it,
fighting back an eye roll and dropped the pill into
her mouth.

"Open please," the nurse said.

I'm going to strangle Kelsey for this.

She moved the pill under her tongue and
opened her mouth.

The nurse shook her head. "Lift your
tongue."

Yeah, I'm definitely going to kill that girl.

Zoey closed her mouth, stared at the
nurse for a second, then gulped down the pill.

She opened her mouth again, this time
lifting her tongue. "Ah, see I swallowed it.
Happy?"

The nurse walked back to her corner,
satisfied and Kelsey let out a loud
condescending laugh from her table.

Ignore the crazy... I am not like her.

Zoey finished her dinner quickly, then
went back to her room just before the dizziness
from the medication started to hit her.

CHAPTER 14

DEC 24th

8:00 A.M.

Between the Christmas music playing from down the hall and Destiny's bubbly voice, Zoey woke up and instantly felt aggravated.

"ZO ZO! Merry Christmas Eve!"

Destiny was sitting at the edge of her bed, with a huge smile on her face.

Zoey looked at the clock as she struggled to sit up.

I'm never taking my bed or my apartment or peace and quiet for granted ever again.

"Come on! Let's get breakfast! I can do your makeup after if you want!" Destiny squealed.

She was dressed in red and green long-sleeved pinstripe pajamas with perfectly matching makeup. Her lips shined of bright red gloss, which were outlined with a dark red lip liner. Her eyelids popped of dark green eyeshadow while her cheeks were decorated in the color rosy red.

"Uh, maybe Destiny," Zoey said, rubbing her eyes.

She felt the bandages on her hands scratch against her eyelids and she shook her head, still angry with herself.

This is my own fault… I can't believe I did this to myself.

"Ugh," Zoey whipped the blanket off her legs and swung them to the edge of the bed.

Destiny's smile washed off her face and she lowered her head.

"I'm sorry, Zo Zo… I didn't mean to upset you."

Zoey shook her head. "No, no… it's not you, Destiny. I'm just really, really frustrated that I'm still in this hospital!"

Destiny rested her head on Zoey's shoulder. "I always try to make Christmas the best I can… but it's just never been the same without grandma."

She moved her head off Zoey's shoulder, fell back on the bed and loud out a deep sigh.

"That's why I want to do a good dance number tomorrow! I just want to do something different… I used to dance all the time with grandma…"

Here I am complaining about missing a boring non-celebratory Christmas at home alone when Destiny's spent who knows how many Christmases in the hospital...

Zoey jumped off the bed and pulled Destiny up by her hands.

"You know what? Get up! Let's go show everyone how pretty you look, Destiny."

Destiny's eyes lit up at the sound of the word *pretty.*

"Okay!" she cheered and leaped off the bed, already on her way out the door.

Zoey refilled her camera with the last set of film she had and then followed her.

As they got closer to the cafeteria, the music that Zoey first heard when she woke up became audibly louder and when they walked in, they spotted the cafeteria nurse controlling it from her tablet with a set of speakers nearby. Few patients were already eating at their tables, bobbing their heads to the tunes. Tina and Lisa were dancing around while Derek thrashed his arms and feet wildly in the air nearby.

"It looks like he's being attacked by a bee," Destiny remarked.

"You're exactly right," Zoey shook her head.

"Welcome to Christmas in the Palace," Destiny laughed.

Welcome to my worst nightmare.

The girls got their breakfast and then sat down with Lisa and Tina, who were now out of breath from dancing.

"Merry Christmas eve, ladies!" Destiny smiled as she patted her hair and outfit, obviously trying to get attention to her look.

"Those pajamas are awesome!" Lisa cheered.

Zoey took a bite of one of the sausage patties on her plate and immediately gagged.

Just as she looked up from her tray, the cafeteria nurse was approaching with the pill bottle.

"Would you like to take your pill this morning, Zoey?" she asked.

Dr. Hall told me I only need to take it once a day. Maybe if I sound honest and ask to take it tonight, maybe she'll forget to give it to me later…

"Uh, can I choose to take it tonight? I think, I think I'm fine right now," Zoey hesitantly asked.

The nurse surprisingly said okay, gave Destiny her medicine, and went to sit back down.

Minutes later, Dr. Hall walked in and announced that the patients could go outside all day as a special treat since it was Christmas. But that was only if the weather stayed cooperative. Nearly all the patients in the room eagerly scarfed down their breakfast and headed out to the courtyard, including Zoey, Lisa, Tina, and Destiny.

Right as they were heading down the hallway, Zoey heard Alex's voice.

"SIS! WAIT FOR ME!" she called out from behind her.

Oh, thank god.

Zoey swung her head around to see Alex hurrying towards her with a tote bag in hand.

"Alex is welcome to come outside with us, Zoey," Dr. Hall said as she held open the door.

They walked outside and sat in the corner of the yard on the grass. Zoey looked through the bag that Alex brought and pulled a package of instant film, three pairs of underwear, a bra, and more outfits out of the bag.

"Is that the right film for the camera they gave you? It said instant in front of it.… I wasn't sure," Alex said.

Zoey felt like crying for some reason, so she did everything she could to hold back her tears.

Crap... I'm being emotional again.

"Yes, it is actually, thank you," she smiled as she wiped away a tear.

"No problem! So, what happened to your hands?" Alex looked curiously at her. "Did that girl mess with you again? Where is she?" she asked as she began scanning the courtyard with her eyes.

"No, no it wasn't her, well... yeah she did mess with me but that's not how this happened," Zoey sighed. "I got mad and hit the carpet... I know... I know. It was dumb of me. I didn't even do it on purpose, I swear. I just got REALLY angry and I needed to let it out... I didn't even realize I was hurting myself until I was done."

Instead of scolding or judging Zoey, Alex gave her a sincere look.

"Well, I hope this doesn't make you stay longer here... just don't do it again! Okay? I know you can get through this. "

Zoey nodded. She knew that Alex was right.

"Anyway, I'm glad I got the right film. I totally guessed at it," Alex said, changing the subject as she tried to take Zoey's mind off things.

"I figured," Zoey sighed.

"You know what?" Alex leaped up to her feet. "Let's dance!"

Zoey looked at her peculiarly. "Uh, what did you just say to me?"

"I said, let's dance!" Alex repeated firmly.

Now Alex has lost her mind too.

"I'm not dancing... especially to this Christmas music... I don't want to look like Destiny," Zoey said as she watched Destiny twirl around the courtyard.

"No, you're not going to look like her. You're going to look better! Come on! Just try it, let's try to get your mind off things," she urged.

"I'm not dancing right now! You're crazy!" Zoey hissed.

"Then I'll dance by myself!" Alex laughed.

Alex began moving her hips side to side as her torso moved along with them. She threw her hands into the air and clapped in between steps.

"Don't make me break out into a twerk!" she warned.

Zoey looked around embarrassed. "Are you crazy, you can't start twerking here!"

"Oh, you better stop me cause I'm about to do it!" Alex sang out as she dropped down into a squat position and Zoey immediately fell to her knees, laughing.

"I can't control it, I can't, I can't!" Alex repeated as she now had one leg in the air, still dancing.

Zoey was now laughing so hard; tears fell down her face. Alex pulled her up from the grass and Zoey began dancing along with her.

Not long after, Dr. Hall walked over to them with a skeptical look on her face.

"I'm sorry girls but you cannot dance like that here. I don't mind the dancing but just," she put her hands up as if to stay calm, "not like that."

Zoey and Alex both nodded and smiled.

As soon as she walked away, they both busted out into hysterical laughs.

"I think she actually found us funny," Alex remarked.

The nurse, who was controlling the music from the other side of the yard, changed the song and they continued dancing (in a more appropriate fashion). Destiny, Lisa and Tina joined them, and they all danced together while taking pictures in between with Zoey's camera, until the visiting hour ended.

Zoey said goodbye to Alex and went back to her room, slamming her door shut behind her. Now that Alex left, a wave of sadness crept back upon her, followed by a burst of rage. Her hands were shaking, and she couldn't control it.

"I told you to keep the door open," Tee's voice startled after he opened the door.

"Yeah, yeah I know," she muttered.

"Door stays open," he repeated and walked away.

Zoey sat down in the farthest corner of the room with her notebook. She re-read over her notes for what seemed like the hundredth time and her thoughts began to wander.

Christmas is tomorrow… I've spent the last two weeks trying to remember something that I might never fully remember or even understand...

Everything began to overwhelm Zoey, and she could feel the anxiety in her grow.

The clock in her room showed half an hour until lunch was scheduled to be served. So, she took a shower, changed into sweatpants and a tank top, then headed to the cafeteria with her camera.

As soon as she got there, she spotted Lisa biting her nails. She was trembling in her seat, so Zoey walked over to her before going to get her food.

"What's wrong, Lisa?" she asked, not prepared for anything she was about to say.

"Kelsey took one of my babies!" Lisa cried.

Zoey turned around to see Kelsey sitting down at another table, holding Lisa's doll.

This is probably a job for Tina, not me.

"Where is Tina?" Zoey asked.

"She's still sleeping," Lisa said through sniffles. "She-- she's going to kill Kelsey when she finds out."

Not if I Kill her first.

Fists balled up at her sides, Zoey marched over to Kelsey.

"What is your problem?" she demanded.

Kelsey purposely took a slow bite of her turkey sandwich and chewed with her mouth open. She swallowed slowly, then took an even slower sip of water.

Zoey leaned over the table with one knee on the bench.

"If you don't put that bottle of water down, I'm gonna slap it out of your mouth, myself!"

"I'm gonna slap it out of your mouth," Kelsey mimicked as she put her water bottle back on the table.

Zoey reached over in one swift move and snatched the doll out of Kelsey's lap.

"Don't take things that aren't yours!" she warned.

Kelsey's mouth fell wide open, speechless.

"That's what I thought," Zoey laughed, then walked back to Lisa's table.

"Thank you so much, Zoey!" Lisa shrieked in excitement when Zoey gave her back the doll. She cradled it tight. "I'm sorry baby."

Now I'm saving baby dolls for adults. Oh, what has happened to me?

1:30 P.M.

After lunch, Zoey went back to her room to take a nap but the noises from the other patients only allowed her to sleep for about ten minutes.

I can't believe I'm still here.

She got out of bed and went over to her nightstand to pick up the photo of the Davis family.

"Christmas... what a happy holiday," she muttered while she held it in her hands.

As Zoey looked at the family, memories of Christmas from her childhood came flooding back to her; the kind of memories that she had not thought of in a long time.

She pictured her mother decorating the tree with garland, along with the painted ornaments they made together, her father stringing the lights strategically around the tree, Christmas music blasting throughout the house.

If only I could go back in time...

Zoey looked at Mrs. Davis and thought of her running towards the bathroom during the photoshoot.

Mom did the same thing when I was ten.

Thinking about Mrs. Davis made Zoey think back to her mother getting sick one Christmas morning. It was their family's first Christmas in Florida. Zoey could remember the excitement she felt when she woke up early that morning, to open her presents. But her excitement had quickly vanished when her mom woke up terribly ill. It took a near two hours to get through opening five presents as her mom kept running to go throw up in the bathroom repeatedly. Zoey had waited every time for her to come back so she could watch her open each one.

She shook her head, pulling herself away from that memory and brought her attention back to Mrs. Davis. The more she examined the photo, suddenly the setting of it started to become clear in her memory.

I left right after she got sick… it was still raining… then I… I went to the cemetery…

"OH MY GOD!" Zoey gasped out loud.

Almost at once, she suddenly began to remember the photoshoot, then leaving after Mrs. Davis got sick. As she continued staring at the photo, Zoey could picture herself driving through the rain with tears falling down her face, making it hard for her to concentrate on the road. Then suddenly, she could remember sitting in front of her mother's grave.

*I miss you… I can't do this anymore…
they were just like us. I want to be a family
again…*

The recollection of her cries nearly
paralyzed her and without realizing, Zoey was
now gripping tightly onto the edge of the bed,
nearly crumpling the photo.

*I was so mad at that family… I went to the
cemetery right after. It was getting dark out…*

Zoey grabbed her notebook out of the
nightstand and began writing:

**I WENT TO THE CEMETERY AFTER
THE SHOOT AND HAD A MELTDOWN.**

**I THINK I WAS UPSET AFTER SEEING
THE DAVIS FAMILY.**

**I HAD TO BE THERE FOR AT LEAST
AN HOUR CAUSE THE SUN WAS GOING
DOWN.**

*If I went to the cemetery after the shoot,
then why the hell would I think that I saw my
mom alive later that night? I didn't go to the cops
til late at night…*

Zoey's chest felt tight, and she started
feeling hot. The more she remembered parts of
her day, the more questions she kept coming up
with and she just could not take it anymore.
Again, she felt a panic attack coming on.

*I need to stop thinking… I need to get out
of this room.*

It was five minutes past two in the
afternoon, so she grabbed her camera and
decided to go to the activity room.

As expected, when she arrived, Christmas music sounded around the room. Lisa and Derek were dancing to the tunes and Kelsey skipped around the tree, while Jonathan paced the room.

Destiny came twirling over to Zoey as soon as she saw her. She was wearing new makeup: glossier and greener than before.

"I changed my look! You like?" she asked, giddily.

"Looks like you're in the... spirit..." Zoey pressed her lips.

Destiny laughed and twirled away towards the TV.

"Got to practice, tomorrow's the big day!"

Zoey sat down at the arts and crafts table with Tina, who was intently focused on a small holiday puzzle. She picked up a wooden tree ornament and began painting it. As she painted the tree green, she thought of painting ornaments with her mother. They would sit at their kitchen table and paint them for hours. Zoey had not painted like that since she was a child and the memory of it made her sad.

Never thought I'd be doing this again...

When she was done painting, Zoey got up from the table and hung the ornament on the Christmas tree, then stood back to admire her work.

"I just put an ornament on a tree... an ornament that I painted... I haven't done that since I was a kid."

She shook her head, not realizing that she just spoke out loud.

"Do you miss doing that?" Dr. Hall asked.

Oh, perfect timing.

Zoey was so lost in thought that she did not notice Dr. Hall standing next to her until she heard her speak.

"Uh, what are you doing here?" she questioned back.

"I thought we'd have a little time for group circle today... just ten minutes with anyone who wants to join," Dr. Hall said.

Like it's really our choice...

Dr. Hall signaled to Debra to turn the music down while she pulled a chair to the middle of the room.

"Merry Christmas Eve! Gather here for group circle please," she announced.

Zoey pulled a chair over to the circle and sat in between Destiny and Tina's chairs.

"Holidays are tough these days... how is everyone feeling?" Dr. Hall asked.

No one answered so she turned her attention to Will. "Will, how are you feeling today?"

"I feel the same as always. Like I don't belong here," he said with his arms firmly crossed at his chest.

No, YOU DO belong here. I DO NOT.

"We feel like we don't belong here either," Derek said sadly, "not in this world... we belong in another," he lifted his head, "another world out there, another planet."

"Who else feels like they don't belong? Not just here but in the world? Do you feel like you're different from others?" Dr. Hall asked.

A few other patients, including Destiny and Lisa, raised their hands. Zoey, Tina and Will, were among the few that didn't raise theirs.

Dr. Hall continued to talk for ten more minutes before letting everyone go off on their own for the remainder of activity time.

"Let's take some pictures, Zo Zo!" Destiny urged as she began dancing to the music that Debra happily turned up.

It's not like I have anything better to do...

Zoey crouched down to the floor and began snapping photos of Destiny, Lisa, and Tina who posed awkwardly and danced around together.

Shortly after, Derek invited himself in and Zoey snapped a photo before switching with Tina, who ended up talking her into being in at least one picture. She reluctantly gave in, not really one to be in front of the camera, and then sat down at the table with the photos as she watched the girls continue to dance and decorate each other in garland and tinsel. Although the girls looked happy, watching them made Zoey start to feel sad again. She began thinking about the few Christmases she had with her parents, and it reminded her of when she used to enjoy the holidays.

As she watched the girls smile and laugh, Zoey began to wonder if she would ever feel genuinely happy around the holidays again.

4:30 P.M.

Zoey laid under the small hospital blanket in her bed. Her thoughts were heavy as she kept thinking about that Christmas morning when she was ten. She tried to think about other holiday memories but the more she forced herself, the more she began thinking about the bad ones. She closed her eyes and let her thoughts wander back to the Disney memory she told Destiny about.

Mom was in a wheelchair so we were able to jump the lines on all the rides... but then she got sick, and we couldn't stay as long as we wanted... so we went back to our RV...

Wow, I forgot about that.

Tears began to fall from Zoey's eyes when she realized that she had completely forgotten about the RV. They would vacation in it in different states when she was younger, during the times when her mother's cancer was in remission. She pictured their large RV and thought about the very last trip that they had taken in it.

We went to New York. That was one of the best Christmases I ever had because I got to see all those lights in the city for the first time... My grandma was there. I think that was our last real Christmas together... before we started spending them in the hospitals...

She wiped away her tears and went to the bathroom to wash her face with cold water.

She lifted her head from the sink and looked at her dark circles and puffy cheeks through the mirror.

"I WILL GET OUT OF HERE. I'M STRONGER THAN THIS," she told herself, then took a deep breath, and left for Dr. Hall's office.

5:00 P.M.

Zoey sat uncomfortably in the chair across from Dr. Hall.

"I-I don't normally talk about my feelings," she stammered.

Dr. Hall nodded, "It's okay. Take your time. I'm here to listen."

"So... I was thinking about my parents, and I think... I think that I repressed a lot of good memories with them because when I go to think about any memories at all, I always think of bad ones... and I think that's because I have more bad ones than good ones. My mom was sick basically my whole life as a kid," Zoey paused, "I know that I have good memories... but the only thing that I can remember that was good, is the last time that we went on vacation but nothing really specific about it."

"Oh yeah, well what was that like?" Dr. Hall asked.

"We went to visit my grandma in New York during Christmas. I remember that I really enjoyed it because I saw all the decorations and lights in the city... and well because I saw my grandma too, I guess."

"That sounds like a very good memory, Zoey," Dr. Hall smiled. "Did you see your grandma often as a child?"

"Yeah... but that stopped right after my mom died." Zoey unintentionally rolled her eyes.

"When was the last time you talked?" Dr. Hall asked.

"Uh..." Zoey paused as she thought about it, "I don't know... I think maybe last year.

Come to think of it, I don't even remember the last time I saw her. She used to fly to see me all the time... I guess I never realized until now that our relationship kind of grew apart after my mom died," she sighed, "along with the rest of my family."

"Do you miss those relationships with your relatives?" Dr. Hall asked.

"I guess... I don't know. I don't really want to talk about it. It's like I said, I haven't spoken to anyone in years... I haven't thought about any of this until now."

And I'd like to keep it that way...

Dr. Hall smiled. "Life changes Zoey."

"Yeah, I know. I must adapt and overcome situations. I have to learn to live with the change," Zoey muttered.

She rolled her eyes and Dr. Hall raised her eyebrows.

"Oh, I'm not mimicking you. I-- I'm just getting tired of being here. I want my normal life back..."

"You're making incredibly good progress, Zoey," Dr. Hall remarked. "I'm happy with how far you've come."

"Okay... but I've been here two weeks already and I still can't remember exactly why I thought I saw my mom, let alone why I went to the police, claiming she's alive... I feel like an idiot. I'm on video... people that know me have seen it! I just can't believe it, but I know it's real because I obviously did it..." Zoey's voice trailed off as she grew more anxious. Tears welled up in her eyes.

"You just might not remember everything, Zoey," Dr. Hall paused, "or you might remember it weeks down the road from now... or maybe days or months. You need to count on focusing on yourself, how to handle your emotions, and how to let the things that are out of your control, go."

Zoey shook her head. "But that's really scary that I still can't remember. What happens if I don't remember at all? Are you ever going to let me go home? What if this happens again?"

"That's why you are here, Zoey. So, we can make sure that what you did does not happen again," Dr. Hall said, softly. "I noticed that you were taking pictures with the girls. You looked happy. You're getting there Zoey. Just a little more patience. How are your hands feeling?"

Zoey swallowed as she thought about hurting her hands.

"They're fine... I think I can take the bandages off now. They don't hurt anymore..."

"I want you to think about your hands next time you feel anxious or mad, okay? Hurting yourself is never the solution," Dr. Hall said.

I think I've learned that by now...

"Yeah... I guess," Zoey groaned.

"Stay strong and positive, Zoey. Everything will be okay, I promise," Dr. Hall smiled.

Easy for you to say.

6:30 P.M.

When Zoey sat down next to Destiny in the cafeteria with her plate of turkey and mashed potatoes, the nurse immediately got up from her chair.

"Ugh, she already spotted me. I was hoping she'd forget that I didn't take it this morning," Zoey groaned.

As she began plotting a way to hide the pill, the nurse started to approach her with the pill bottle in one hand and an iced coffee in the other. The nurse took a sip of her drink before giving Zoey the pill and just as she did, an image of a woman drinking coffee suddenly flashed into Zoey's mind.

In the next moment, she could remember standing barefoot downtown at night, staring at that woman, who was sitting on the bench. She was with another lady, both sipping on their drinks in front of Zoey's favorite coffee shop. The rain began to fall, then they got up from the bench and started to jog away.

That's when Zoey ran right after them. She could now remember the puddles splashing in between her bare feet. Rain mixed with her tears as she began calling out to the woman.

I thought that… that was my mom…

Zoey pictured herself stumbling up the slippery steps to the police station while she frantically asked random people to help her find her mother. Then she remembered the police officers face behind the front desk as she demanded for her help.

Zoey's body was now shaking tremendously in her seat at the cafeteria.

"That's when I pushed the papers off the front desk, and they brought me into that room... then I started demanding... oh my-"

"What are you talking about? Would you like your pill or not?" the cafeteria nurse asked as she tapped her feet against the floor.

"Uh, I- I- I-" Zoey stammered as she could not properly form any words.

Her body and mind were frozen with the memory of the woman downtown.

"That wasn't... that wasn't my mom..." she muttered.

"Zo Zo, it's okay," Destiny consoled her.

Tears flowed down Zoey's face, and she began hyperventilating.

"I need assistance," the cafeteria nurse said into her radio.

Zoey's body was so paralyzed by her new memory, that she never felt Tee pick her up minutes later and take her back to her room.

CHAPTER 15

DEC 25th

5:00 A.M.

Zoey sat at the edge of her bed, hyperventilating. Everything that she did on the tenth and had forgotten about all this time, began to resurface all at once, as soon as she woke up.

Oh my god, oh my god... I remember... that-- that woman wasn't my mom... I woke up that morning... I was tired. I barely got any sleep the night before because I was updating my computer all night... which is why I woke up an hour later than I was supposed to... and that's why I was late to the Davis shoot. How could I forget that? It started raining as soon as I got to the photoshoot... I left after the star broke and the shoot lasted only two hours. That's when I drove to the cemetery... that family made me sad... then I went home to work on the photos. I was frustrated... not just because of the sequins but because I was mad at the Davis family... They reminded me so much of my own... then I went for a walk downtown...

Zoey felt like her head was going to explode as she started to replay that night in her head.

It was around 10:00 p.m. when she had sat down in front of her laptop with a glass of wine and started going through the photos of the Davis's that night. She could now clearly remember feeling frustrated and crying as she looked through them. She felt so irritated, that she started to feel a panic attack coming on and in a moment of frustration, she had abruptly grabbed her purse and stormed out of her apartment, forgetting to put her shoes on. It was dark out, just before businesses were about to close. She walked around the small city aimlessly as people passed by, giving her odd looks when they caught sight of her shoeless feet. The rain had come tumbling down as soon as she stepped outside, which is when she saw the woman on the bench.

Who the hell did I see? That-- that wasn't my mom...

Zoey was holding onto the edge of her bed in the hospital so hard, that the bandages on her hands were beginning to come off.

"I need air... I need air..." she gasped as she pulled the bandages off her hands.

She marched out of her room, down the hall towards the door that opened out to the courtyard and tried opening it, impatiently.

"Excuse me, what are you doing?" a nurse who happened to be walking by, asked.

"I need air," Zoey gasped as she continued to try to pull open the locked door.

"Okay, okay, calm down… deep breaths," the nurse said.

"NO! NO! No deep breaths! I need real air," Zoey insisted.

"As soon as breakfast opens, you'll be allowed to go outside all day just like yesterday. That's in less than two more hours. Do you think you can handle it until then?" the nurse asked, calmly.

I can't handle another second in this place.

Zoey took a moment to inhale and exhale deeply.

Instead of arguing, she nodded in agreement then went back to her room and sat on the floor, frozen by all her new memories.

7:00 A.M.

As soon as the clock hit 7:00 a.m., Zoey was the first one waiting in front of the door to the courtyard. A nurse opened it for her, and she happily ran outside to sit on the bench, thankful to be the only patient there.

The sun had just risen and there was a light breeze in the air. Zoey closed her eyes and thought of the woman that she ran after, and she shook her head as the vivid sound of her pleas made her cringe.

I really thought that woman was her… I called out to her… I was confused…

Zoey pictured the innocent woman's face, who looked almost identical to her mom. She was smiling next to her friend on the bench, laughing just before the rain started to fall.

What was I thinking?

"Have you had breakfast today?" The nurse who let Zoey outside distracted her.

"Um, no…" Zoey muttered.

The nurse suggested that she should eat something, so Zoey reluctantly went back inside the hospital. But instead of going to the cafeteria, she went straight to Dr. Hall's office.

"Dr. Hall!! Are you in there yet?" she knocked rapidly on her door.

Dr. Hall opened the door a moment later, wearing a red business skirt and satin blouse, clearly in the holiday spirit.

"Good morning and Merry Christmas, Zoey!"

"Yeah, yeah Merry Christmas… uh, can we talk?" Zoey asked, anxiously.

Dr. Hall looked at her watch. "Just for a few minutes. I just stepped in my office. Are you okay?"

"Yeah… that's fine," Zoey quickly walked in and sat down.

"What's going on this morning?" Dr. Hall sat across from her.

Zoey shifted in her seat and took a deep breath. "Well… I uh," she hesitated, "I remember everything now… everything I did on the tenth…"

Her eyes began to well up with tears as it was hard to get the words out.

"Take your time honey," Dr. Hall said in a reassuring tone.

"So, I went to visit my mom at the cemetery after I left the photoshoot. I was upset because the family that I photographed reminded me of my own family... Then... I went back home, and I guess I started to edit their photos later on that night, but I got frustrated so I went for a walk," Zoey paused, "and I saw this woman on a bench and I- I- I guess I just... I thought she was my mom. She looked just like her... I don't understand why I thought it was her..."

Zoey stopped to take a breath as her face was now covered in tears.

"It's okay. I'm glad that you can remember all that now. You should be too," Dr. Hall said as she clasped her fingers together on the desk.

"Remember when we spoke about stress and how it can cause a lapse of mem-"

"-memory. Yes, I remember," Zoey finished her sentence, wiping away the tears.

Dr. Hall nodded, "I believe that between daily stress and not grieving your mother properly is what caused you to have a breakdown, Zoey."

Zoey shook her head. "You're telling me that my brain broke for a day?"

Dr. Hall smiled. "No, it didn't break. You just needed a break. That's probably why you went for a walk. Your brain was subliminally telling you to relax. I'm incredibly happy that you remember everything now." Dr. Hall got up and walked over to Zoey.

She put a hand on her shoulder and said, "this is progress. Keep practicing the anxiety techniques, okay? Especially now."

Zoey nodded, emotionless.

"I'm sorry, I have a session with another patient in a few minutes and I have to get their notes ready. I'm glad you came to talk to me," Dr. Hall continued. "I know you've been focused on remembering your day and now that you did, try to focus more on how to handle your emotions about it. Do you understand?"

I understand that you're really never going to let me leave this place.

Zoey got up silently, forced a smile, and walked out of the room.

2:00 P.M.

After leaving Dr. Hall's office, Zoey cried herself to sleep. It was a few minutes past two in the afternoon when she finally woke up. She missed lunch but oddly didn't wake up hungry and instead, felt sick to her stomach.

As soon as she sat up, she felt queasy and immediately ran to the bathroom to throw up. After a few minutes of what seemed like an eternity of dry heaving, she was finally able to sit back on the floor and catch her breath. She counted to thirty in between deep breaths before getting up to her feet and forcing herself to get into the shower. She stood under the lukewarm water until it turned cold. When she dried off, she dressed into sweatpants, and a big shirt.

Just as Zoey was about to crawl back in bed, Tina opened her door.

"Alex is on the phone for you. I answered it as I was passing on my way to session," she said.

"Thanks," Zoey muttered and left to go to the hallway phone.

When Zoey heard Alex's voice, she instantly burst out into tears.

"Calm down! What's wrong?! What happened?" Alex asked, frantically.

It took Zoey a few minutes before she could solidly utter anything understandable.

"I remember see--seeing my mom or think--thinking I saw her," she stammered as she continued to tell Alex everything she could.

After she was done explaining, Alex said that she would come by that night, and they were going to figure out how to get her out of there. She even demanded to talk to Dr. Hall, but Zoey would not let her as she didn't think bothering her would help the situation.

"At least you remembered! Imagine not remembering ever. Imagine completely forgetting and never figuring out how you ended up in the hospital... it's nothing to be ashamed of. What Dr. Hall said makes sense. I know you don't like what happened but now that you can remember everything, now you can leave. You can handle yourself... I know you can."

Through sniffles, Zoey tried to agree, and Alex reminded her to stay strong before they said goodbye.

Zoey went back to her room to get her camera and then went out to the courtyard. When she walked outside, there were a few patients already dancing to the Christmas music that blared from Debra's portable speakers. Destiny, who wore a thin long-sleeved red dress, now had a Santa hat on as well, as she twirled around the grass practicing her dance. Lisa and Tina were doing cartwheels nearby and Johnathon, who wore antlers on his head, paced the yard per usual. Kelsey was sitting in the grass, laughing to herself. She was also wearing antlers and Miriam sat on the bench alone, oddly wearing a Christmas sweater. Zoey snapped a photo and waited for it to develop as she watched everyone linger around.

"Afternoon everyone, Merry Christmas!" Dr. Hall called out as she walked into the courtyard.

Behind her, followed Tee. He was carrying a large box similar to the donation's box from the other day. He set it down on the bench next to Miriam who promptly slid away and told him to leave her alone.

"Merry Christmas to you too, Miriam," Tee grinned, then walked away smirking.

"I have one last holiday surprise for you all…" Dr. Hall pointed to the box. "You each get one gift again but this time, I want you to choose one for someone else and that person will choose one for you!"

The only person who seemed excited about this game besides Dr. Hall was Lisa, who jumped up and down gleefully with her dolls.

Dr. Hall had everyone pick a present, starting with Lisa who happily volunteered. She picked out a board game and gave it to Tina, who reached in the box and then pulled out a newly packaged Halloween makeup kit. Lisa gasped in excitement, and nearly cried from happiness.

When it got to Zoey's turn, she pulled out a plastic children's tiara and gave it to Destiny, who was very satisfied with her choice.

"You know what a queen deserves, Zo Zo! Nice work girly!" she said as she placed it carefully on her head, acting as if it were truly made of gold.

Then she pulled out a sticker book and gave it to Zoey.

"Here! You can decorate your pictures with these!"

"Thanks," Zoey muttered as she took the book from Destiny.

After picking out gifts, Zoey sat in the grass to enjoy the sun and fresh air while she could. She spent the rest of the hour distracting herself by doing yoga and taking photos of everyone. Eventually, her thoughts started to become overwhelming, so she left the courtyard and went back inside the hospital, hoping to find something else to take her mind off things.

Just as she passed the activity room, she decided to turn around and go inside. A nurse was sitting in place of where Debra normally did, and three other patients were playing board games at the table. Zoey walked over and stood in front of the Christmas tree and stared at the little ornament she had painted the day before.

I never thought I would end up here.

It wasn't until the nurse in the room touched Zoey's shoulder, that she realized her face was filled with tears. Her body was numb, and her feet felt stuck to the floor.

"Can I get you anything?" the nurse asked.

"I-- I'm fine," Zoey tried to manage her composure as she wiped her eyes, but the tears continued to flow.

"I'm going to put a movie on for you, okay?" the nurse said and gently led her over to the couch.

Zoey slowly sat down and stared at the screen for the next hour until the nurse reminded her that it was time for her session.

5:00 P.M.

"How's the rest of your Christmas going, Zoey?" Dr. Hall asked.

"Please don't remind me that it's Christmas," Zoey groaned.

Dr. Hall pressed her lips together in a half-smile. "I'm sorry, Zoey. I know the holidays are rough on you-"

"No, what's rough on me is the fact that I'm stuck here," Zoey sobbed. "I-- I know what I did wasn't... normal. I get that now. When will you let me leave?"

Dr. Hall typed something on her laptop for a moment then looked at Zoey.

"Do you think this will happen to you again?"

God, I hope not.

Zoey shook her head. "No, I don't think so... I mean, I know that I lashed out... I recall that now."

She rolled her eyes at the thought of her actions.

"Why the eye roll?" Dr. Hall asked.

"Because I shouldn't have done that. I'm an adult. I acted like a child… it's embarrassing," Zoey spoke low.

"You were confused, Zoey. You were distraught," Dr. Hall said. "Between it being your mother's birthday not long ago, the holidays and the family that you photographed reminding you of your own, are all the reasons for what caused your mental breakdown. It's okay to acknowledge that."

Zoey sighed as that was all she could muster up.

"You have a lot of pent-up anger inside of you and I believe that comes from when your mother died. It's understandable. I am glad that you are remembering now. This is a good step… so now I want you to focus on that source of your anger," Dr. Hall said.

Zoey rubbed her eyes and temples, wishing she could just disappear.

Dr. Hall leaned in on her desk and gave her a sincere look.

"Zoey, I don't think you ever took the time to really grieve your mother when she died."

Zoey looked up through tears, "wh--what do you mean?"

"You lost your mother at a very young age, and you never spoke to anyone about what you experienced until just now, with me," Dr. Hall said. "It's understandable not wanting to talk about it, especially when you were a teenager… And you didn't only lose your mother; you lost the rest of your family along with her. When you spoke to me about your relatives, you spoke with aggravation and sadness in your voice. You have never grieved losing them either. Grief isn't always about death."

"I-- I guess," Zoey stammered.

Zoey had not realized until now that Dr. Hall was right. She had never spoken about her family in the way she has with Dr. Hall to anyone, ever in her life. The realization shocked her as she felt both confused and relieved at the same time.

"I don't think you realize this Zoey, but you are a very strong woman to have seen and gone through what you went through... especially at such a young age, and to be where you are in your career, that's amazing. But besides work, have you ever taken any time for yourself? Have you ever done anything that you wanted to do just for fun?"

"I took a week off of work a few months ago but that's it, really," Zoey shrugged.

"And what did you do during that free week?"

Zoey looked down at her lap as she thought about it.

"Uh, not much. Just kind of sat at home, went out to eat with Alex once... stayed home really. I didn't mind it. I slept a lot."

"Your mind and body need to rest and I'm not talking about sleeping. They both need to breathe. I strongly suggest that you do seek some type of grieving therapy when you get home," Dr. Hall said.

Zoey's eyes lit up. "Are you saying I can leave now?"

Dr. Hall smiled. "Not quite."

It's time I figure out an escape plan...

Zoey slumped back down in her chair and groaned.

"I want you to keep practicing those anxiety relief strategies on the paper I gave you. Your problem is not only with anxiety, but it is with anger too. You have a lot of built-up aggravation in you that you have never dealt with, which comes from the loss of your mother. You need to learn how to manage your emotions and cope with her death before something like hallucinating your mother happens again," Dr. Hall said.

"The woman looked just like her... but it wasn't her," Zoey mumbled.

"It'll be okay, Zoey," Dr. Hall smiled. "I want you to think about what you can do for yourself when you go back home. I know you have clients and I know that these past two weeks of losing them didn't help you and it's causing you more stress... but you need to learn to cope with that stress and take time off work. After you handle what you need to do in work, I suggest that you plan for at least a few days to do something that you enjoy... whether you go shopping, to the beach, get a hotel for yourself, take a small road trip... anything Zoey, anything that you think will make you happy. If you focus on that, the rest of your hospital stay should fly by like a breeze."

If only it could fly by today...

"Okay, I'll think of something," Zoey mumbled and left the office, then headed back to her room.

Just as she was closing the door behind her, Destiny showed up in front of her.

"ZO ZO! Get your camera! You're going to miss my dance!"

She stood there in a velour green shorts and jacket jumpsuit with rosy cheeks, gold eyelids, and red glossy lips. Zoey sighed and grabbed her camera, then followed Destiny towards the cafeteria, who happily skipped down the hall.

When they got there, Christmas music played, and for once, the room was filled with more patients than Zoey had ever seen before. She went in line to get a plate filled with turkey, mashed potatoes, corn, and a soda, then went over to sit with Lisa and Tina, who were both wearing red Santa hats as they chomped on their turkey. Destiny went over to the cafeteria nurse instead of sitting with them.

Just as Zoey took her first bite, the song *All I Want for Christmas* came on through the portable speakers.

"Mm- mm- mm," Destiny cleared her throat as she twirled herself to the middle of the room. "If you all will turn your attention to your highness!"

She began to twirl dramatically with her arms loosely in the air and Zoey pulled out her camera to snap a quick picture.

Destiny slid around the room with her arms to the side, as her movements seemed to be more improv than rehearsed. Jonathan, who had been sitting at a table, abruptly stood up and flipped his tray just as she spun behind him. The sound startled her, causing her to lose balance and she instantly dropped to the floor.

"JOHNATHON! YOU FREAK!" she hissed as she stood back up and brushed herself off.

"Destiny's about to flip her-"

Just as Tina was about to finish her sentence, Destiny picked up the turkey that had fallen on the floor from Johnathon's tray and chucked it at him fiercely.

"AHHHHH! AHHHHH!" he screamed, then bolted out of the cafeteria into a run.

"Destiny, enough!" the cafeteria nurse called out from her chair.

Destiny marched over to the girl's table angrily and plopped down next to Zoey. "Ugh!" she slammed the table with her palms which reminded Zoey of the police station.

What's done is done... don't think about it.

"Relax, Destiny," Tina said. "You don't want to spend Christmas in your room, you know that."

"I WANTED TO SPEND CHRISTMAS SHOWING YOU ALL MY AMAZING DANCE BUT THAT STUPID SCHIZO MESSED ME UP!" Destiny shouted. She stood up with her hands on her hips.

"I'll see you lovelies later. I have a bone to pick with that man!"

She stomped away, clearly on a mission to mess with Johnathon.

Zoey watched Destiny storm out in a rage and wondered if she looked like that in the police station.

"I probably looked worse," Zoey mumbled.

"You're doing that talking to yourself thing again," Tina laughed.

Zoey ignored her, finished eating, then went back to her room, sick of the same routine that she's been repeating for the past two and a half weeks.

1:00 A.M.

Alex had come to visit later that night and urged to speak with Dr. Hall, but she was already gone for the night. The hour passed quickly and after she left, Zoey laid wide awake in bed, trapped in the horrifying memories of herself on the tenth.

Try to focus on myself... do something for myself when I get out of here.

As she thought back to her conversation with Dr. Hall, Zoey realized she hadn't ever really had a vacation in her life. Truthfully, she never thought about it or ever thought she needed one. The realization of stress and not taking time to grieve her mother's death are the reasons of why she ended up in the hospital made Zoey cringe.

"I never want to end up back here again," she said to herself as she closed her eyes and thought about Dr. Hall's suggestions.

I don't think I can afford a road trip... but I can go to the beach...

It wasn't until now that Zoey realized how much she took living ten minutes from the beach for granted.

She began thinking about the sound of the waves crashing against the shore and her feet sinking in the sand. Her mind began to ease itself and eventually, she fell asleep sometime around one in the morning.

CHAPTER 16

DEC 26th

8:00 A.M.

It felt like a 50-pound weight had fallen onto Zoey's chest when she woke up. She started to feel a panic attack coming on so she immediately started taking deep breaths.

I can't let that happen again… I'm stronger than this… All I need to do is take a break… this will never happen to me again… I won't let it.

Instead of being hung up on what she did that got her in the hospital, she decided to focus on what she could do to get out of it. After taking a few deep breaths, she took a shower, then left her room and went to get her breakfast.

She walked into the cafeteria and got her food, then the nurse gave Zoey her pill as soon as she sat down across from Destiny. Zoey swallowed it and immediately started shoving her face with food, hoping it would help weaken the effects of the pill.

If I just follow the rules for the whole day and act like I'm fine… maybe, Dr. Hall will let me go… I already admitted that I went crazy… what more can I do to get out of here?

She took bites of her scrambled eggs and toast until there were only crumbs on the plate. Although she started to feel dizzy, Zoey did her best to fight it and stay with Destiny until she finished eating.

Just as they were leaving, Zoey noticed the nurse writing something on her tablet.

Hopefully, she's writing something good in my chart.

"I'm so mad at Johnathon!" Destiny pouted as they walked through the hallway.

"I'm sorry you didn't finish your dance… but the beginning of it looked pretty cool," Zoey said as she weakly followed a foot behind.

It wasn't until they looped around back to the cafeteria, that Zoey realized she had been following Destiny aimlessly around the hallway. "Where are we going?" she asked.

"Mm, not really sure… but thanks for interrupting," Destiny laughed.

Zoey laughed too and it was just in time as Dr. Hall was walking by.

"Hello ladies," she smiled at them.

"Morning, Dr. Hall," Destiny fake smiled and looked her up and down.

"Morning Dr. Hall!" Zoey tried to say in an upbeat voice, like Destiny's as she forced a smile.

"Zoey, how are you feeling today?

Like I'm ready to get out of here…

"I'm doing great actually!" Zoey said.

"That's great to hear. You seem like you're in a good mood. Have you thought about what you are going to do for a break when you go back home?" Dr. Hall asked.

"Yes, actually I have. I think I'm going to spend a few nights in a hotel on the beach… like you suggested," Zoey said as she thought about waking up to the sound of the waves.

"I've taken the beach for granted for too long. I barely go there. I think I'm going to change that when I leave here," she paused, "you know when you think I'm ready, that is..."

"That's a great idea. I'll see you later during group circle," Dr. Hall said.

Hopefully, that'll be the last you see of me.

Zoey nodded, still painfully holding a fake smile until Dr. Hall turned away.

"If you want to be more convincing, try not making your face look like that," Destiny remarked.

Zoey dropped her smile and rolled her eyes.

She's probably right.

2:15 P.M.

When Zoey got to the activity room, Dr. Hall was already sitting in a circle with the other patients.

"Look what the cat dragged in!" Kelsey laughed.

I can do this... ignore the crazy.

"Good afternoon, Kelsey," Zoey swallowed.

"Okay everyone, let's talk about how we are feeling today. Who wants to go first?" Dr. Hall asked.

Zoey looked at the circle of patients who were all sitting quietly. She took a deep breath.

"Uh, I'm feeling better today. I remember what happened to me and… I feel quite relieved now."

Although she was aggravated by her actions, Zoey knew that what happened to her was serious and from that moment on, she vowed to herself that she was never going to let her emotions get the best of her again. Now in order to get out of the hospital, she needed to make Dr. Hall know that.

"Oh yeah? Tell us more!" Kelsey annoyingly asked.

"Uh, I thought I saw my mother in the street… I thought I saw her sitting on the bench," Zoey paused and looked at Dr. Hall, "but I know that was not her now. I guess it was another woman that looked like her… I know my mom is still dead."

"But why did you think you saw her?" Kelsey pressed.

Do not let this girl get to you…

"Because I was so stressed out, that I guess I just kind of… lost it. I'm learning to take time for myself from now on… I never grieved her when I should have. I guess I've been angry about her death for a long time," Zoey breathed as she looked at Dr. Hall.

Everything she said was true. From that moment forward, Zoey decided she was really going to focus on herself, as Dr. Hall had been suggesting. After the past two weeks of a rollercoaster of emotions, Zoey never wanted to feel them again and she knew her mother would not want her to feel like that either. She had never been through something so scary before.

In fact, it even scared her more than seeing her mother die. The fact that she had forgotten an entire day had completely defeated her. Never in her life had she felt so out of control but now was the time to take it back.

Dr. Hall continued to speak about emotions during the holidays and asked the group more questions. Zoey did her best to answer every one of them, hoping to show an effort of cooperation.

When activity time was over, she went back to her room and laid in bed until it was time for her session. The anger that she had felt these past few days subsided but still lightly lingered in her bones. That was only because, for the first time since Zoey woke up in the hospital, she admittedly now understood why she was there. Tears welled up in her eyes.

I can't cry... I can't get mad... I'll be okay...

She took several deep breaths before summoning up the courage to go to Dr. Hall's office for her session.

5:00 P.M.

When she walked into her office, Dr. Hall was sitting at her desk with a few papers in her hand.

"So, you decided that you're going to go to the beach for a few days, huh?" she asked.

"Yeah, I think so," Zoey said as she sat down in front of her.

Dr. Hall nodded. "So, Zoey do you understand what happened to you now?"

"Yes... yes I do... you're right. I guess, I'm still grieving my mom..."

Zoey looked down at her feet, embarrassed that she let this happen to herself.

"After these past two weeks, you have made exceptionally good progress and I want you to keep making it. I think you are on the right track now," Dr. Hall paused, "Zoey, I believe that you are stable enough to go home."

Zoey sat up straight and gasped, "you-- you're serious?! I can really go home?!"

"I am going to release you with the anxiety medication you have been taking," Dr. Hall said.

"You do not have to take it every day. You should only take it when you think you need it. I want you to work on managing your stress, giving yourself some time to relax, and controlling your anger. You need to keep doing a technique that works for you in the moments you start feeling angry or anxious, okay?"

Zoey was nearly at the edge of her seat.

"Yes, yes! I promise I will do all of that! I never want to come back here again... no offense."

Dr. Hall smiled and handed Zoey the papers that she had been holding.

"I want you to also think about the idea of speaking with a therapist when you need to. Here is a list of a few local ones. These are your discharge papers. You can call Alex to pick you up or if you need a cab, we will pay for your fare."

Zoey felt so relieved that her body felt lighter. As much as she wanted to cry from happiness, she held back the tears and thanked Dr. Hall.

"Thank you! Thank you! Thank you! I promise I will do all those things and you will never see me ever again!" she exclaimed.

Dr. Hall laughed and let Zoey leave the office.

She immediately jogged over to the hallway phone and dialed Alex's number. "THEY'RE LETTING ME OUT!! COME GET ME, PLEASE!!" she cried out as soon as Alex answered.

"Oh great! I knew you would get out of there! I'm checking out at the grocery store right now. I'll head over there as soon as I'm done. This is great! I'm so happy for you!" Alex cheered.

Relieved tears were now falling from Zoey's face as she couldn't hold them back anymore. "Me too! I'll see you soon!"

They both hung up and Zoey skipped back towards her room.

On her way there, she stopped at Destiny's room. She walked in and found her humming while applying bright orange eyeshadow on her eyelids.

"Hey Destiny... so I have news," she said.

"Oh, do tell Zo Zo! News is my favorite category!" Destiny said as she examined herself in the mirror.

"Well, they're letting me go..." Zoey said as she held up her discharge papers.

Destiny dropped the eyeshadow palette and put her hands on her hips.

"Well look at you, Zo Zo! I'm glad for you girly but I'm sad to see you leave. You were one of the coolest people I've met here," she said.

Zoey smiled. "Thanks Destiny... you're uh, you're pretty interesting yourself."

"You must say goodbye to Lisa and Tina! Come, come!" Destiny grabbed her by the elbow and led her out to the hallway.

They went to find Lisa and Tina who were sitting on the floor outside of their rooms, playing cards. Lisa nearly cried when Zoey told them she was leaving so to cheer her up, Zoey took a picture with her and gave it to her to keep, along with the one she took of her and Tina in the hallway days before. Tina on the other hand, didn't seem to care so much as it seemed like she was used to meeting people and seeing them go.

Destiny and Zoey continued down the hall and stopped when they saw Miriam pacing in the hall.

"Hey Miriam, it was nice meeting you but they're letting me go..." Zoey said.

Miriam stopped talking to herself and gave Zoey a skeptical look.

"Good for you kid. Be Careful out there!"

"You too, Miriam," Zoey nodded and continued down the hall with Destiny.

Just before they turned the corner towards her room, Kelsey bumped into Zoey and for the first time, Zoey was excited to see her.

"Oh, Kelsey! Well, it was nice meeting you but I'm getting out of here," Zoey smirked, "have a nice life."

"Ha, you'll be back!" Kelsey laughed, maniacally.

Zoey laughed back as she knew that was not going to be true and went back to her room. Destiny sat on Zoey's bed while Zoey gathered all of her things together. Right before Tee knocked on her door, she took two photos with Destiny and gave her one to keep while Zoey kept the other. Then she took out three photos that she had taken of Destiny's dancing, days before and gave them to her.

"Oh, thank you, Zo Zo! You are the best!" Destiny cheered.

"Your time has come," Tee solemnly said as he stood in the doorway.

Zoey smiled. "I'm now just understanding that you actually love working here. That's why you're so sarcastic."

Tee raised his eyebrow. "You coming? Or not?"

Zoey rolled her eyes and grabbed her things.

She followed him to the front door, along with Destiny who skipped next to her.

"Well Zo Zo, good luck on the other side!" Destiny sighed and gave her a tight hug when they got to the nurse's station.

I might miss Destiny...

"Hang in there, Destiny..." Zoey smiled and walked out of the double doors that she was so badly, hoping to walk out of for the past two and a half weeks.

I'm really leaving this place... I'm really going home...

CHAPTER 17

DEC 27th

9:15 A.M.

The time on Zoey's cell phone showed a quarter past 9:00 a.m. She sat on her couch smiling, happy to be in the peace of her own home. After spending time in a place where she had almost no control of anything, Zoey never wanted to take her freedom like living in her little apartment for granted ever again. In fact, she didn't want to take anything in her life for granted anymore.

The coffee maker in her kitchen beeped, alerting her that it was ready. She got up and walked into the kitchen where the aroma of it filled the room and made her smile.

"Oh, how I missed you," she sighed as she poured herself a cup.

She walked over to the window in her living room with her coffee and gazed out at the busy street in front of her. There was not a cloud in the clear blue sky and the sun shined bright. She looked at the cars driving by and thought of looking out of the hospital window at the courtyard protected by barbed wire and softly chuckled.

I can't believe I went through all that…

Zoey walked away from the window and went to open her purse that she left on the living room table. She pulled out all the photos that she had taken in the hospital and laid them out on the table in front of her.

At least my story isn't as sad as everyone else I met...

Looking at all the people in her photos that she encountered within the past two weeks, made Zoey realize that her life wasn't as tragic as she had always thought. Compared to the rest of the people she met, especially Destiny, Zoey realized that at one point in her life, she was considered lucky. At least she had a good life as a child with loving parents who did their best in everything they could. What happened to her mother was no one's fault, and she had no one to blame which she was just learning now.

Although she was relieved to be home, she still felt a light sense of anxiousness. The nagging feeling of getting her work done hung to her, so she went over to her laptop but then stopped herself from opening it.

Take some time off. Work on yourself.

Dr. Hall's words rang in her head and Zoey instantly thought back to sitting in that small prison-like room with no lock on the door.

Never again...

She opened her laptop and instead of clicking on her client's files like she first intended, Zoey searched for cheap hotel rooms on the beach. After a few moments of browsing through different websites, she booked herself a two-night stay in a hotel right on the coast of the beach. She chose to check-in later that night, then went to pack her things.

3:00 P.M.

While on her way to the beach, Zoey decided to make a quick detour to the cemetery. She sat on the ground in front of her mother's name as she thought about the last time she was there, wailing like a child in the rain.

"I will never let that happen to me again, Mom. I miss you so much. I guess I never grieved you when I should have. I guess I am right now. It's already been ten years. I have gotten this far without you, I know I can get through the rest of life too, even though I don't want to. But I need to... And I know it. I'm going to the beach for two nights to clear my head. You would love it. They have remodeled so much on the boardwalk now; you would not even recognize it."

Zoey closed her eyes to keep her voice from trembling. She took a few deep breaths, reminding herself that it was okay to feel the emotions she was feeling.

"It doesn't matter how many times I remember you being sick. What matters is that you were alive, and you were with me."

Zoey thought back to Destiny crying on her shoulder in the activity room.

"In these past two weeks, I met so many other people who have had it way worse than me. I'm considered lucky to have had you for as long as I did. I know life is always going to be tough, but I have to get through it, and I have to get through controlling my emotions. I already called dad and told him I'm home. He was relieved but I don't think I should've told him what happened. It probably really worried him… but I'll go visit him next week," she sighed and stood up.

She kissed her fingertips and bent over to place her hand on her mother's name. "Bye, mom. I love and miss you so much."

Zoey walked back to her car and drove away from the cemetery, genuinely feeling a sense of relief for the first time in a while.

BOOKS BY THE AUTHOR

FIND THESE BOOKS ON KINDLE, IN PAPERBACK & IN AUDIO.

THE WOMAN I BEFRIENDED: (Book 1 in "THE WOMAN" SERIES): *Several missing men. A suspicious neighbor. A pattern only Ellie sees.*

THE WOMAN I WANT DEAD: (Book 2 in "THE WOMAN" SERIES): *A cat and mouse serial killer thriller.*

HE THOUGHT I WAS HIS: *A psychological stalker thriller.*

EVERYTHING LED ME TO YOU: *A new adult romantic crime mystery/thriller.*

ZOEY'S MEMORY: *A medical mental health mystery.*

WE SHOULDN'T HAVE COME HERE: *A tropical storm thriller.*

THE UNSEEN AND UNINVITED: *A thriller short story on kindle unlimited.*

TWISTED VOWS: *A deadly marriage of lies and revenge.*

You can find Sara Kate's books on Amazon, Barnes & Noble, Walmart, Target, Books-a-million, and other store retailers!

You can also request any of her books to be stocked in your local independent bookstores.

If you enjoyed this book, I'd love to hear your thoughts in a review on Barnes & Noble and Amazon.

Acknowledgments

Thank you to my husband and my father for always being my first readers and honestly giving me their input on my stories.

To my family, anyone who supports me and to those who always buy every single one of my books regardless of whether they read them or not, those who provide honest reviews, and anyone who I force to answer my ridiculous questions to make the settings and characters come to life; I absolutely love and appreciate all of you.

To my ARC TEAM – You are amazing and so patient with me. I am forever grateful for your honesty and promotional work.

About the Author

Sara Kate with a K writes crime fiction, psychological, and survival thriller and mystery books in her RV out of South Florida. Aside from writing, she enjoys rollerblading, photography, painting, and anything thriller/mystery related.

INSTAGRAM.COM/SARAKATEAUTHOR
FACEBOOK.COM/SARAKATEAUTHOR
GOODREADS.COM/SARAKATEAUTHOR
BOOKBUB.COM/SARAKATEAUTHOR